P9-DBY-019

The Rizzlerunk Club

THE BIG
BAD
LIES

The Rizzlerunk Club

THE BIG
BAD
LIES

LESLIE PATRICELLI

CANDLEWICK PRESS

Copyright © 2022 by Leslie Patricelli

First edition 2022

Library of Congress Catalog Card Number 2021946036
ISBN 978-0-7636-5105-3

21 22 23 24 25 26 LBM 10 9 8 7 6 5 4 3 2 1

Printed in Melrose Park, IL, USA

This book was typeset in Bulmer.
The illustrations were created digitally.

Candlewick Press
99 Dover Street
Somerville, Massachusetts 02144

www.candlewick.com

*To every pet who has endured
the* gentle *love of children*

Abby

Lily

Snort

a.k.a. Gail and Leslie Patricelli
and their new puppy, Daisy

Author's Note

Dear Readers,

    The story you are about to read includes a class science project on nutrition involving some adorable white rats. I am not recommending that YOU should use rats for a class nutrition project. When I was in fourth grade at Sunny Hills Elementary School way back in 1979, well, things were different then! Rest assured, no rats were harmed in the writing of this book. Also, no rats were harmed in our class project. (Except for one. Argh.)

Sincerely, your rodent-loving friend,
Leslie Patricelli

Chapter 1
♡ Rats! ♡

Me

**I'm Lily Lattuga and
I L♡VE RATS!** ♡

If you don't love rats, it's probably because you don't know any.

I know four of them!

Last week, we got pet rats in my fourth-grade classroom. Mrs. Larson, our teacher, brought them in for us to do a science project about nutrition. (Don't worry, we aren't going to *eat* them for nutrition, even though that's what my bestest friend, Darby Dorski, thought.)

For the project, we'll keep two of the rats in one cage and feed them only junk food, like chips, soda, and stuff your parents *don't* like you to eat, and the other two rats in another cage, where they'll only get healthy food, like veggies, whole grains, and other stuff that your parents *always* want you to eat.

We're planning to weigh and measure the rats daily to see if their size changes over time. Obviously, Mrs. Larson is hoping that the health-food rats will end up being super rats. But, even if they are, they're going to be miserable. I know, because they'll be eating the same food my mom makes us eat at home. (Our last name is Lattuga, which means *lettuce* in Italian—I guess that's why lettuce is practically all Mom ever feeds us.)

We haven't started the experiment yet. We haven't even named the rats! That's because of what happened last Friday, the day Mrs. Larson surprised us with them. . . .

It's a long story—and it starts like this: Jill Johnson had a *brilliant* idea.

Who's Jill Johnson? Well, she used to be Darby's best friend until she moved to London at the end of third grade. Lucky me! 'Cause when I moved to Sunny Hills Elementary at the beginning of *fourth* grade, Darby needed a new best friend. And guess who it is? ME!

Darby and I have a lot in common:

1. We both live on Pine Lake. (She lives at one end, and I live at the other.)
2. We both love frogs.
3. We both love drawing.
4. We both love candy. (But, duh, who doesn't?)

That's why we're best buds under frogs! We even made our own club—the Rizzlerunk Club (we're the only two members). Darby told me that she didn't mind that Jill had moved, since now she had *me* as a best friend. Plus, she said Jill always got her into trouble with her bad ideas.

Then guess what happened? Jill moved back, along with her bad ideas. And she was very convincing at making her *bad* ideas seem like *good* ideas. One of her ideas (having to do with frogs' eggs and the boys' bathroom) even got me sent to the RTC!

The RTC is where the naughty kids go for punishment. Our mean playground monitor, Mrs. Rash (kids call her Mrs. 'Stache), is the RTC monitor, too.

Jill even took over our Rizzlerunk Club—she named herself our queen! It was like she was a hypnotist, and she'd put us into a trance.

But Darby and I finally woke ourselves up, stood up to her, and started thinking for ourselves again. Things got a lot better for the three of us when we did.

But then guess what happened? After all that, Jill told us she had to move back to London. Her last day of school was Friday—the day we got the rats in our classroom. We were having her going-away party when Mrs. Larson introduced us to them.

And guess who had an idea?

Jill opened the cages and let the rats out. It was chaos! One rat jumped onto Gabriella Nelson's ponytail, which made her friend Tillie scream and pass out. Mikey Frank called 911, and firefighters came. (One of the firefighters was Mikey Frank's dad— Fireman Frank. Mikey Frank is the cutest boy in

school, and all the girls have a crush on him, so none of us were surprised when Mrs. Larson started getting all googly-eyed around his dad.)

Luckily, Darby saved the day! She charmed the rats with food and got them back into their cages. So now everyone is calling her the Rat Whisperer.

And now, today, we finally get to *name* our rats!

"You may tear a piece of paper out of your composition books," Mrs. Larson explains, holding a baseball cap upside down, "on which you may write your chosen name for one of the rats. Please fold your paper neatly when you're finished and place it in the hat."

I pick the name Snowball, which seems perfect, because all of our rats are white, so it would be good for any of them.

"Who would like to choose the names?" Mrs. Larson asks after she has collected all of our entries.

"Me, me, me!" shouts David White.

He stands up and walk-runs to the front of the room. He reaches into the hat and then reads the names: Ratsinburger, Marshmallow, Kevin, and Riley.

"I made up Ratsinburger!" Darby the Rat Whisperer whispers to me.

We decide to name the junk-food rats Ratsinburger and Marshmallow because Mrs. Larson thinks those names sound "appropriate." We name the health-food rats Kevin and Riley, but I decide that I am going to nickname Kevin Snowball, because I think Kevin is a really stupid name for a rat.

Kevin

Then Mrs. Larson tells us the *best* news!

"Our rats can't stay in the classroom by themselves during the weekends," she says. "I have a sign-up sheet for those of you who might like to take care of them. If you're interested, please come to the front of the room in an orderly fashion."

We all rush to get in line. I'm near the front, so I get to take one home in three weeks, but Darby doesn't get to take one home for forever.

"Mrs. Larson!" Billy Ditsch shouts. "José crossed out my name and put his name on the list, but I put my name there first!"

People call Billy Ditsch *Billy Snitch*, because he's such a tattletale.

"Is that true, José?" Mrs. Larson asks.

"Yes," says José. "Because I picked the name Kevin, so I should be able to take him home first."

"Please move your name to the end of the list," Mrs. Larson says to José. "Billy was first."

Billy is smiling and puffing out his chest like he just scored a goal on the stupid select soccer team that he talks about all the time.

"Tattletale," José whispers as he walks back to his seat.

On Friday, Billy takes Kevin home.

By Monday, we only have three rats.

Chapter 2
The *Lily and Darby* File

"Billy, would you like to tell the class what happened to Kevin?" Mrs. Larson asks.

Billy is excited to tell. He stands up in front of everyone.

"I brought Kevin home and took him out of his cage to play with him," he says, "and he got away. He ran into our bathroom, and we couldn't find him. But then my dad heard him behind the wall. He had to drill a big hole under the sink and try to catch him, and he couldn't get him, and then he got his hand stuck. Then he said the f-word!"

"Billy!" Mrs. Larson says. "That last part was *not* necessary!"

"Not necessary" is one of Mrs. Larson's favorite things to say. Darby and I always start giggling when she says it. Now everyone is giggling. Mrs. Larson settles us down in her usual way.

José raises his hand.

"Yes, José?"

"Now we only have one health-food rat!" he says. "How are we supposed to do our experiment?"

"It won't be statistically relevant," says Iris Barton, who spends lots of time in the library.

"That's a good point," Mrs. Larson says, "but we'll still be able to compare Riley, our remaining health-food rat, with the other two junk-food rats. It may not be as accurate of a study, but we should still see similar results. Now, let's move on and take out our history books."

We read about George Washington and how he led the Continental army to overtake the British during the Revolutionary War.

Mikey Frank raises his hand, and Mrs. Larson calls on him.

"Did George Washington really cut down a cherry tree, and then when his dad asked him if he did it, he said, 'I cannot tell a lie,' and told the truth about it?" he asks.

When Mikey talks, half the girls in class blush— especially Darby.

"No one can prove whether the story about the cherry tree is true or not," says Mrs. Larson, "but it illustrates a very important point: George Washington went down in history as an honest man. He believed that honesty is the best policy, and I happen to agree with him!"

Darby and I agree, too. We even say so in our Rizzlerunk Club pledge, which goes like this:

I pledge allegiance to the Rizzles, of the United Club of Rizzlerunk, and to the invisible clubhouse for which it stands, best buds under frogs, with loyalty and honesty for all.

We say our pledge every day when we meet in our clubhouse, which is in the corner of the playground in the dirt. No one can see it, because it's invisible, but I pretend it looks like this:

After we put our history books away, Mrs. Larson lets us draw, which is my favorite thing to do. Darby likes to draw, too. We both know I'm better at it than she is, but that doesn't make it any less fun to draw together.

I have the idea to draw Mrs. Larson, since I love doing caricatures of people. We take turns drawing. I think we nail it.

Suddenly, Billy Snitch is behind us. He reaches down and grabs our drawing.

"Billy, please bring that here," Mrs. Larson says. He does.

"Thank you, Billy," she says.

"You're welcome," he says, smiling.

"You may sit down, Billy," Mrs. Larson says.

As he turns away from Mrs. Larson, he sticks his tongue out at us.

I swallow. My mouth is dry. *Not the RTC again!* Before, I thought it was Jill's fault that I went to the RTC, and now it is my own bad idea that might get us sent there!

"This really *isn't* necessary, is it, girls?" she says. "You shouldn't be drawing pictures of me like this. It's disrespectful. Do you have anything to say for yourselves?"

"Sorry," we both say.

"Do I really have a mustache?" she asks, smiling a little.

"No," we say.

"Girls, I am going to put this drawing into my file cabinet." She pulls out a file folder and labels it neatly: *Lily and Darby*. "Let's make it our goal to have this be the only item that will be in it. Okay?"

"Are we in trouble?" Darby asks, sounding as scared as I feel. "Are you going to call our parents?"

"I don't think that's necessary," says Mrs. Larson, "but I expect you to use better judgment from now on."

I watch Mrs. Larson close the drawer and hope that I never see that file again.

Chapter 3
I Cannot Tell a Lie

The next day, we have a surprise in class—a new student!

"Another one?" I whisper to Darby. "But Jill just left!"

Mrs. Larson introduces him: "Class, this is Deets Frizzle."

Darby and I both giggle. Frizzle rhymes with Rizzle.

Deets Frizzle is tan, like a perfectly cooked marshmallow. He must not be from around here, because here in Issaquah, it's almost always raining.

"Deets, would you like to tell the class a bit about yourself?" Mrs. Larson asks.

"I'm from Florida," says Deets. "I have a brother who's in seventh grade and a pet shih tzu named Princess."

"Mrs. Larson! Mrs. Larson! He just said the s-word!" says Billy.

Everyone laughs.

"Billy, please," Mrs. Larson says, shushing him. "Class, a shih tzu is a breed of dog. You may continue, Deets."

"We just moved from our big house in Florida to the biggest house on Pine Lake," he says.

shih tzu

"I live on Pine Lake, too!" Darby says. "I live in the oldest house on the lake."

"I live in the newest house," says Deets.

Darby is looking at Deets the same way she looks at Mikey Frank. Does she like him or something? He doesn't seem very likable to me.

"Thank you, Deets," Mrs. Larson says. "You may sit down."

Deets sits down right next to Darby in what used to be Jill's seat. I see her sneaking peeks at him all morning.

At first recess, Darby and I go to our invisible clubhouse. It's sprinkling, but our clubhouse is under the trees, so the dirt isn't wet. We do our Rizzlerunk handshake and say our Rizzlerunk pledge.

"Look at Deets over there," Darby says. "He's *so* cute."

"It looks like everyone else thinks so, too," I say.

He's surrounded by lots of kids, including Gabriella, Sonja, and Tillie, who have their own club called the Gabbys.

"We should invite Deets to be part of the Rizzlerunk Club," Darby says. "Since Frizzle rhymes with Rizzle."

"I don't think so," I say. "We already tried having a three-person club with Jill, and she took over. I like having a two-person club. Plus, he brags too much."

"I know, isn't he great?" says Darby.

After recess we do math. I write a new equation on the side of my worksheet:

Next, we have science, and we get to weigh and measure the rats. This is the best part of our experiment, because we get to hold them and they're so cuddly.

"I have rats at home," Deets tells everyone. "They're bigger than these rats. Smarter, too.

They can do all kinds of tricks. I trained them to walk on two legs like people!"

Everyone looks at Deets like he's the coolest boy they've ever seen. Mrs. Larson looks kind of annoyed.

"I'm not sure about that. These rats are really, *really* smart," Darby says. "I should know. Everyone calls me the Rat Whisperer. I'm a natural with rats."

"Not as natural as me," Deets says.

But when Darby tries to hand him Ratsinburger, he pulls his hands away.

We take our seats and enter the weight data into our science journals. So far, nothing is happening to the rats as a result of their different diets.

"Rats are omnivores, just like us," Mrs. Larson tells us. "Does anyone know what an omnivore is?"

"Omnivores eat a diet of both plants and animals," Iris answers. "I could be an omnivore, but I *choose* to be a vegetarian."

Iris

"Interesting, Iris," Mrs. Larson says. "As humans, we can make the choice to follow different types of diets. Can you tell us why you've chosen to be a vegetarian?"

"My whole family is vegetarian," Iris tells us. "We do it to help the environment. Did you know one pig farm makes as much waste in a year as about twelve thousand humans? So, instead of hot dogs, we eat veggie dogs, and instead of bacon, we eat Fakin'."

I like Iris, but she's weird. I can't imagine not eating bacon! I love bacon. And what the heck is Fakin'?

By next recess there's a thunderstorm, and it's pouring down rain.

"Rainy-day recess," Mrs. Larson says. "You may read a book or do a quiet activity in the classroom, or you may go to the gym."

Almost everyone goes to the gym. The only kids left in the class with Darby and me are Iris, whose face is hidden behind a thick book, and Billy, who's building a card house with division flash cards.

"Let's draw!" I say to Darby, getting out my pens and some paper.

First we play heads and bodies. That's a drawing game we made up, where one person draws the head and neck, while the other person isn't looking, then folds over the top of the paper, and the other person draws a body. The drawings turn out pretty funny.

Then Darby has an idea.

"Let's draw Deets and me in the tunnel of love," she says.

"I thought you liked Mikey!"

"I do, but now I like Deets better."

"But you don't even know Deets!"

"I know," Darby says. "He's mysterious."

We draw a masterpiece.

"It's so romantic!" Darby whispers.

I pretend-gag.

While Darby starts coloring in the drawing, I go to use the bathroom.

When I come back, I see Mrs. Larson standing behind Darby. She's tapping her foot, like our caricature of her would do if it was animated.

"Darby, I would like to have a word with you at my desk, please. Now!" she says, confiscating the drawing.

Uh-oh.

Darby gets up and starts to follow Mrs. Larson to her desk. I'm terrified and I don't move.

For a second, I consider sitting back down and pretending I had nothing to do with the drawing, but then Darby would get in trouble and I wouldn't, which wouldn't be fair, since we both drew the picture.

I think about George Washington and the cherry tree. He didn't *have* to tell his dad about the tree. His dad wouldn't have been able to prove he did it. But *he* knew he'd done it, and I'll bet he would've felt bad for lying.

I decide to be like George. I make myself walk over to Mrs. Larson's desk. My feet feel like they have Mom's ten-pound ankle weights attached to them.

"Yes, Lily," says Mrs. Larson.

"I drew it, too," I say.

"Thank you for your honesty, Lily," Mrs. Larson says. "Girls, you need to know that it is *not* okay to draw pictures of the other students in the classroom, just like it was not okay to draw a picture of me. It's disrespectful."

Mrs. Larson pulls open her file cabinet. She takes out the *Lily and Darby* file and puts our cartoon on top of the caricature we did of her.

"I know you both love to draw, and you are very creative, but as I said before, I expect you to use much better judgment about what you choose to draw in class. I was hoping that we wouldn't have to add to this folder. Now, *please* make an effort to draw pictures appropriate for the classroom so we don't have to see this file again."

"Okay," we both say.

We stand there nervously.

"You may go to your seats," she tells us.

"Thanks, best bud," Darby says as we walk to our desks.

"Honesty is the best policy," I say.

Then we do part of our secret Rizzlerunk handshake—the Rizzle Sizzle—sit back down, and take out our math worksheets. Because no one ever gets in trouble for doing math.

Chapter 4
Rizzle Fizzle

At lunch the next day, Darby wants us to sit by Deets instead of in our normal spot, but he's already surrounded by all the other kids, and there's no room for us except at the end of the bench. We squeeze in and take out our lunch bags.

I turn mine over and dump it out. Mom packs the *worst* lunches!

Darby usually packs her own lunch since her mom goes to work early—and she has better food to work with than I do.

"I'll trade you a Pop-Tart for half your sandwich," she says.

"You don't have to," I say. "It's peanut butter and alfalfa. Yuck!"

"Yum!" says Darby.

"If you say so," I say, handing her half my sandwich.

Darby starts eating quietly. I see her looking at Deets, who seems to be telling a story to everyone, because they all look amazed.

"We should invite him into our club before he gets a bunch of other friends," Darby says.

"I think he already has a bunch of other friends," I tell her.

When we walk out to recess, Darby finds Deets standing with most of our class surrounding him. I can hear him telling them that he had a pet tiger cub in Florida!

"That can't be true," I whisper to Darby.

"How do you know?" Darby says. "Maybe he lived at the zoo."

Darby walks right up to Deets and looks at him. I would never walk up to anyone in front of a big group of kids, because of my super-shyness, but Darby never worries about what anyone thinks.

"Hey, Deets," Darby says, "do you want to be in our club? It's called the Rizzlerunk Club, and since Rizzle rhymes with Frizzle, Lily and I thought you should be in it."

"Cool," Deets says. "I was in a club in Florida."

"Sweet!" Darby says.

Oh, no!

"We were called the Tuffs, 'cause we were the toughest kids in our school," Deets says. "I was the president. So, I'll be the president of your club."

"But I'm the president," Darby says.

"I'd be a better president," Deets says.

All of a sudden Darby doesn't look so excited about Deets.

"I'm the president," she says, and walks away.

I follow her, relieved.

"You can be president of the Gabbys, Deets," I hear Gabriella say.

"He *is* a liar," Darby says. "A club for the toughest kids in school? That sounds made up. And a *tiger* for a pet? Maybe he'd have an alligator for a pet in Florida, but a tiger?"

"Told ya," I say.

"Who would believe that stuff, anyway?" Darby says.

We turn around and look at Deets again. He's surrounded by even more kids, including fifth-graders!

"I guess everyone but us," I say.

"And me," says Iris, who has quietly appeared beside us.

Darby and I jump.

"Right," Darby says. "We're all too smart."

I want to remind Darby that just a few minutes ago she'd believed *everything* Deets said, but I don't.

"Iris, you should be part of the Rizzlerunk Club," Darby says.

I like Iris, so this time I think maybe a third person isn't such a bad idea.

"No thanks," Iris says. "I'm already in a club. The Nobody Club. There's nobody in it but me! But you're welcome to join if you like."

"Oh," says Darby as we walk back into our classroom. "No thanks. But let us know if you change your mind."

Chapter 5
Bacon

After school, Darby comes to my house on the bus. Darby usually comes to my house instead of me going to hers, because she says my house is like a library and hers is like a zoo.

That's because even though Darby and I both have one sister, she also has two brothers—and all three of them are as wild as chimpanzees.

Darby likes my sister, Abby, even though I think she's annoying since she's so smart and knows way more about almost everything than I do. Plus, she collects all sorts of weird things.

We get off the bus with Abby and walk along a muddy path toward our house. We pass our neighbor's dog, Zach. Zach is a scary Doberman pinscher. He barks, growls, and drools at us every morning and every afternoon when we walk by. Luckily, he's behind a very tall cyclone fence.

"Zach is even scarier than the ghost of Captain Rizzlerunk," Darby says.

Captain Rizzlerunk was the captain of a ship that sank in a storm on Pine Lake a long time ago—or at least that's what Darby told me. Darby tells lots of stories, and some sound *really* made-up. But her dad is writing a book about true ghost stories, so it makes sense she would believe them. My dad, on the other hand, tells me ghosts can be explained by quantum physics, whatever that means, so I don't know *what* to believe.

Zach is charging at the cyclone fence and trying to jump over it. He almost reaches the top. Drool is dripping from his sharp teeth.

"What'll happen if he gets out?" Abby asks me.

Zach Snacks!

We make it home alive and walk through the mudroom door, take off our wet clothes, and hang up our backpacks, like Mom trained us to do. I hear Mom before I see her.

SOOO-EEEEY!

Why can't I just have a normal mom who asks, "How was school?"

"Mom, why are you saying that?"

"Because," Mom says, "we've got ourselves a pig!"

"I thought we couldn't have pigs," Abby says.

Mom wanted a pig when we moved here, but then we found out that our house was too close to the lake to have one. Anyway, Abby and I thought our dog, Snort, was good enough.

Snort

"Well, Abby," Mom explains, "your teacher, Mrs. Swanson, raises pigs on her property. She and I were talking, and she said that we could buy a pig and keep it at her place! She lives near you, Darby. They picked up three piglets today, and one of them is ours. As soon as

Dad gets home, we'll go over to see it. Right now, let's have some veggies for snacks! We can bring the trimmings over to feed the pigs."

"Hooray," I say, using what Mom calls my talent for sarcasm. "Veggies for snacks."

Finally, Dad comes home. Mom greets him at the door with a bucket of kitchen garbage. It's the same bucket that we have to empty onto our compost pile every night.

"Let's go see our pig!" she says.

We all pile into Vanna, our minivan, including Snort. The compost is sitting between Abby and me. It's filled with coffee grounds, eggshells, rotten banana peels, and a stinky old onion . . . topped by the fresh celery tops from our so-called snack. It smells disgusting. I can't believe the pigs are going to eat it.

We pull up to Mrs. Swanson's house, and Abby, Darby, and I jump out of the car like it's on fire and take giant gulps of fresh air. Darby helps me carry the big white bucket around the side of the house to the pigsty.

Mom yells:

SOOO-EEEEY!

Abby and I look at each other and giggle. Mom just sounds really dumb yelling that. It works, though. Three adorable little piglets come running to the trough.

CUTE ALERT!

They're so cute! They're about the size of Snort (which is perfectly pick-up-able), but pink with curlicue tails and little pink snouts. One has a brown spot right on the top of its head. Dad opens the fence, and we go in. They come running up right around our legs. Mom bends down and pets one.

"Awww, they're so soft!" she says.

"Which one's ours?" I ask.

"This one with the spot," she says, picking it up like a baby.

"Let's name it Wilbur!" Abby suggests.

"No way," I say. "Probably every pig in the world is named Wilbur."

"How about Lily Junior?" Darby suggests.

"Ha ha, very funny," I say. "I am *not* a pig."

"Yes, you are!" says Abby.

I give her a Sister Glare. Friends are allowed to say stuff like that. Little sisters are not.

"They really shouldn't be naming it," Dad says quietly to Mom. "We don't want them to get too attached."

"What does that mean, Dad?" I ask.

"Nothing," he says. "Except we might want to name him Bacon."

"What? You mean we're gonna eat him?" I ask.

"Oh, honey," says Mom, "we eat pig all the time. You love bacon! This will just bring us closer to our food. Instead of getting our bacon in a plastic package, we'll get it right from the source."

"But I prefer a plastic package. I don't want to meet my food before I eat it."

"I don't want to eat him, either," Abby says. "I'm going to be a vegetarian."

Mom dumps the compost on the ground, and the three pigs start chowing down.

"He eats this, and we're going to eat him?" I ask. "This whole thing is really grossing me out!"

"It is a little unappetizing," Dad says. "I may agree with the girls, that I'd rather see my bacon on my plate than on the farm."

"I like the name Bacon," Darby says. "It's to the point."

We all agree that Bacon is a pretty good name for a pig.

Dad takes a bunch of pictures of us with Bacon, and then we drive away.

On the way out of the neighborhood, we see a U-Haul truck parked in a driveway. A kid is trying to pick up a big box, and a man is standing there pointing at him. It looks like the man is yelling.

"That's the bully kid!" says Abby. "He pushed over a first-grader at recess and I saw it. Then he lied to Mrs. 'Stache and said he didn't do it and he didn't even get in trouble!"

"That's Deets!" I say. "He's a new kid in our class."

"That man yelling at him looks mean," Darby says. "Do you think it's his dad?"

"I don't know. I hope not," I say. "He sure looks like Deets, though."

Suddenly, a little furry dog with a ponytail on top of its head runs up to the man, barking.

"What a cute little shih tzu!" Mom says.

The man spins around and glares at the dog. We all gasp, because he looks like he might do something horrible, but Deets quickly bends down and picks up the dog and runs inside.

For a second, I feel sorry for Deets, but then Darby reminds me what a liar he is.

"He said he lived in the newest, biggest house on Pine Lake!" she says. "That's just a normal house, and it's not even on the lake! He really *is* a liar. We should tell everyone at school. The only thing that's true is he really has a shih tzu!"

Abby starts giggling.

"Shih tzu!" she says.

"You should try being nice to that kid," Dad says.

"Yeah, but he's a bully," Abby says.

"And a liar!" I add.

"Well, you might try," Dad says. "It doesn't look like he gets much kindness at home."

Chapter 6

How Many Lies Can You Tell?

The next day when Mrs. Larson calls roll, I notice she doesn't call Deets's name. Maybe he got moved to a different class. I wouldn't mind that.

But then we watch SHTV, the school news station that we watch every morning. The fifth-graders get to run it, so usually only fifth-graders are on, but when it starts, our class is surprised to see Deets on the screen, too!

"Hey!" José says. "How come Deets gets to be on SHTV?"

"Because he's a new student," Mrs. Larson tells us. "The fifth-graders invited him to be on."

"That's not fair!" says Ethan Jackson.

It's true — it's not fair. I didn't get invited on SHTV just because I was a new student! I'm not jealous, though. Being supershy and being on TV don't go together.

Deets starts by reading the weather.

"Hi, I'm Deets Frizzle," he says. "Today's weather will be fifty degrees with a light drizzle."

The two fifth-graders start laughing.

"Drizzle rhymes with Frizzle!" one of them says.

Deets glares at them. They stop.

"I'm from Florida. I had a huge house on the beach there. And a pet reef shark! I just moved here into the biggest house on Pine Lake. I have a brother and a shih tzu, but I had to leave my shark in Florida."

"A pet shark?" Darby shouts. "He said he had a pet tiger! And he didn't say anything about trained rats. We shouldn't believe *a word* he says."

43

"Darby, enough," says Mrs. Larson, raising her eyebrow.

I guess Darby won't have to work too hard to convince everyone that Deets is a liar. It's pretty obvious. But when Deets comes back to class, everyone is asking about his shark.

"Dude, you had a *shark*?" Ethan asks.

"I have a shark-tooth necklace," Gabriella says, holding it out for Deets to see.

"I have one, too," says Deets, showing her his. "Mine's bigger. It's from a megalodon."

"Cool," Gabriella says.

I roll my eyes at Darby.

Once we're settled, we get to write and draw in our journals for twenty minutes. I draw a picture of Mom that looks like this:

I look over at Darby's journal and see a picture that looks like this:

Darby is good at lots of things, but drawing isn't at the top of the list.

"What's that?" I ask her.

"They're my cows, Tootsie and Roll," says Darby. "We had them when I was six, until my parents slaughtered them."

"They did that?" I ask her.

"Yeah. They stored Tootsie and Roll all chopped up in the freezer in our garage. There are still a few pieces in there that we never ate."

"You ate them?" I ask.

"Of course we ate them. Mom and Dad served them for dinner. Obviously, I wasn't happy about it. It was murder! They'd make me go out to the garage to get the meat. The pieces were wrapped in white paper and labeled with things like 'Tootsie Flank' or 'Roll Tongue.' But I have to admit, they tasted pretty good."

"We have to save Bacon!" I say. "Maybe we could sneak him out of his sty in a pillowcase, then let him go in the woods."

"That could work," Darby says. "But we should wait until he's old enough to take care of himself."

"It's a plan," I say. "Rizzlerunks to the rescue!"

After recess, Mrs. Larson fills us in on a new geography project.

"As part of our curriculum on the earth," she says, "you will be doing a report on the seven continents. You may pair up with a partner for this assignment."

Darby and I look at each other. We get to do a report together!

"I'd like one handwritten page on each continent," Mrs. Larson continues. "You will get extra credit for illustrating your work with either drawings or photos."

Ethan raises his hand.

"Yes, Ethan?"

"I went to South America once," he says.

"Can you tell us any interesting facts about South America?" Mrs. Larson asks him.

"Yes!" Ethan says. "Everywhere we went in South America, I could get a McDonald's Happy Meal!"

cajita Feliz

¡Yo soy muy feliz!

"Interesting, Ethan," Mrs. Larson says. "But in your report, I'd like you to focus on culture and facts *specific* to South America and the other continents."

"I've had a Happy Meal on all seven continents," Deets says.

"I'll bet he hasn't even left the country," Darby whispers.

At recess, Darby and I decide to jump rope instead of having a Rizzlerunk meeting. Darby starts singing as we jump.

Hey, Deets Frizzle, before the last bell. How many *lies* can you tell?

I look at Deets, and he's surrounded by kids as usual. He's obviously lying again because their mouths are all open in amazement. I know I should try to be nice to him like Dad says, but he makes it way too hard. So I join Darby.

"Four, five, six, seven . . ."

Deets ignores us. Darby stops jumping. I get tangled in my rope, so I stop, too.

"We need to tell everyone what a liar Deets is," Darby says. "That we saw him moving into his house, and his dad was yelling at him, and he doesn't even live on Pine Lake!"

"Maybe we should leave out the part about his dad," I say. "My dad said we should be kind. Besides, we don't even know if it was his dad or not."

"I'll bet it was," Darby says.

"Well, you say it," I tell her. "I'm too chicken. What if everyone still believes him and not us? I mean, if they believe he has a pet shark, they might."

"I'm not too chicken," she says. "We need the truth!"

Then she yells,

I immediately pull my sweatshirt hood over my head to hide.

"Deets Frizzle, the new kid—he is a liar! L-I-A-R! Lily and I saw him moving into his new house yesterday, and he doesn't live in a big, new house, and he doesn't even live on Pine Lake!"

Everyone stops what they're doing and looks at Deets.

"Really?" says Ethan.

"No! Not really!" Deets says. "It was my uncle's house. I was helping him move in."

"It was his uncle's house, dumb Darby!" says Billy.

"Dumb Darby!" says Gabriella. "You're jealous."

"Am not!" says Darby. "It's true. He's a liar!"

"I like the nickname Dumb Darby," says Deets, smiling. "That's *way* better than the Rat Whisperer."

Chapter 7
Exposed!

After school, Darby comes over, and we're excited to start our continent report. We go into the den to use the computer, but Mom and Dad have it turned off, and they changed the password so we can't log on without permission. We start looking through their old *National Geographic* magazines instead.

"This is a gold mine of information!" Darby says. "I don't think we even need the computer!"

Darby and I find issues of *National Geographic* that have pictures from every single continent. There are photos of people from different places around the world—and some of them aren't wearing any clothes!

Next, we find an article about Italian Renaissance art, and pretty much everyone in that art doesn't have any clothes on, either. We cut out a picture of Michelangelo's statue of *David*. David was a normal guy who fought a giant named Goliath with a slingshot—and guess what he was wearing? His birthday suit! Then we find an article about Japanese baths, and the people in the baths aren't even wearing bathing suits!

"I think we have a theme!" I say.

Pretty soon we have a great collection of fascinating people from all over the world. The people in Antarctica have clothes on because it's so cold, so we cut out pictures of penguins and polar bears instead.

"This is going to be better than Deets's fake report about all the places he's probably never been," Darby says.

We get some plain paper for our report. We can't find any glue, so we make paste out of flour and water. We decide it would be prettier if it had a color, so we add blue food coloring, which gets all over the paper.

"Let's paste in the pictures first, then do the writing," Darby says.

Pretty soon there are so many pictures in our report that there isn't room for very much information, so we squeeze in little bits where we can—mostly stuff we already know, like *Antarctica has penguins and lots of ice.*

"Our report is looking really blue," I say. "And the paste doesn't work that well."

The magazine pictures are so wet with paste that they get all warped, so when they dry, they are kind of crusty and wrinkled.

"It adds texture!" Darby says.

When we're all finished, we look at our report.

"Do you think she'll mind that there are so many people without clothes on?" I ask Darby.

"Well, that's what it's like," Darby says, "or there wouldn't be so many pictures about it!"

On Monday Mrs. Larson makes a sour face when she looks at our report, and I *don't* think she's trying not to laugh this time. She calls us over when we're just about to head out to recess.

"Darby and Lily," she tells us, pointing toward our report, "these photos in your report are completely inappropriate."

"But those were the most interesting pictures we found for the continents," Darby says.

"I'm sure you found these photos interesting. I know I wasn't very specific about what to include in your report, but—"

"You said to make it creative!" Darby says.

"Yes, I did."

"Well, it *is* creative!"

Mrs. Larson's sour face

"Yes, that is true," says Mrs. Larson, "but you girls don't seem to be learning your lesson about what's appropriate for class and what isn't."

"But they're from my parents' *National Geographic*s," I tell her. "How were we supposed to know they weren't appropriate?"

"Well, I think you might have guessed by the lack of clothing," she says. "It is very important that you understand that you are not being sensitive or respectful to these people of different cultures by choosing to highlight only their nudity rather than—"

"But that's what was in the articles!" Darby interrupts.

"I'm sure that the text in the articles had much to say about their specific cultures. I am expecting you to use *much* better judgment when you redo this."

Then she opens her file cabinet and tries to slip our report into the *Lily and Darby* file, but the papers in it are so thick and crunchy that she has to take out the file and bend the bottom of it so it will hold more. Now ours is the thickest file in her cabinet.

"Redo it?" we both say.

"Girls, besides being insensitive and inappropriate, your report contains hardly any information about the continents themselves, and some information you do include is incorrect. Polar bears do not live with penguins in Antarctica. Polar bears live in the Arctic. On top of that, your report is a mess! I'm afraid if you don't redo it, I will have to fail you on this project."

"An F?" I say, terrified.

"Yes. An F," she says. "*If* you don't redo it."

"So . . . we should only show pictures of places where people wear clothes?" Darby asks.

"I think that would be wise," Mrs. Larson says.

Chapter 8
Contrapposto

LILY DARBY

After lunch recess, we have some free time for drawing.

"Let's draw Michelangelo's *David*," Darby says. "I'll bet I can draw it better than you!"

"First of all, I can draw it better," I whisper. "Second of all, are you crazy? No way! We *just* got in trouble for putting naked people into our report. There are three things in our folder now, and so far she's been nice about it. But if you count the caricature we did of her and the cartoon of you and Deets, this was probably our third strike, and three strikes, you're out."

Darby looks at Mrs. Larson, who is correcting papers.

"She's busy," Darby whispers. "And what's the big deal, anyway? All those Italian artists made everyone naked back then. Their art was so much better than the Dutch art where they were all wearing weird hats and prissy collars."

"True," I say, "but she said we need to learn our lesson about what's appropriate, and Michelangelo's *David* probably isn't, considering she didn't like it in our report."

"I've been practicing drawing him," Darby says, starting to sketch. "My drawing's going to be better than yours!"

That's it. My drawing will be better and I know it. Despite my better judgment, I start drawing, too.

We put our heads down and our arms around our papers. We know we aren't

Dutch Darby

being suspicious, because we usually draw like that. I'm kind of nervous, but then I get pretty into it and forget all about Mrs. Larson.

I draw *David* standing *contrapposto*, which I learned about from the article. It means that his weight is almost all on one leg, so his hips are kind of tilted. It's not bad! I do lots of shading, and I'm pretty impressed with the result.

"Wow, that's a good drawing!" Darby whispers, peeking over my arm. "It looks just like him! I guess you win."

I look at Darby's drawing.

I try to be quiet, but I can't help but laugh a tiny bit.

I wouldn't guess that it was the *David* statue, except that he's holding a slingshot and is definitely in his birthday suit.

We both burst out laughing at Darby's drawing.

"Darby and Lily, do you have something you'd like to share with the class?" Mrs. Larson asks, giving us a look over the top of her glasses.

"No," we both say at the same time.

"Well, please don't giggle unless you're ready to share what's so funny," she says.

"What are we thinking?" I say to Darby. "We could get in *so* much trouble!"

I fold up my drawing and quickly tuck it into my pocket. Darby crumples hers up like garbage and pushes it into her desk, along with a million other pieces of crumpled-up paper. Then we get out clean paper and draw more pictures.

When I get home from school, I show Abby my drawing.

"Michelangelo's *David*!" she says. "Nice *contrapposto*. But Mom and Dad probably won't like it."

Abby must be the only seven-year-old in the world who knows what *contrapposto* is, except maybe in Italy. I'm proud of my drawing, but maybe she's right that Mom and Dad might not appreciate it.

I admire my picture one more time, then bury it in the garbage so no one will ever find it.

Chapter 9
The Teeny-Tiny Lie

On Friday, Mom picks me up from school. It's already my weekend to take home a rat! Darby and I put all the supplies in a box and pick up Riley's cage. Deets walks up next to us.

"What a wimpy rat," he says. "My rats are stronger."

"No, they're not," says Darby. "I'll bet you don't even have rats."

"So what if I don't?" says Deets.

"Well, you can't just *lie*," Darby says. "People don't like liars."

"Everyone likes me," says Deets.

"Riley doesn't like you," Darby says. "I can tell. I'm the Rat Whisperer."

"Does too, Dumb Darby," Deets says.

"Does not!" says Darby. "See how he's bruxing and boggling. That's 'cause you're here."

Bruxing is when rats grind their teeth, and boggling is when their eyes pop in and out, but usually it means they're happy. Deets probably doesn't know that because he probably doesn't really have rats.

"Does too!" says Deets. "Say it, Darby! Riley likes me!"

"No, he doesn't!" Darby says.

Deets kicks Darby in the shin.

Bruxing and Boggling

"Ow!" Darby shouts. "Fine. He likes you, you big bully!"

"What's going on?" says Mrs. Larson, coming up behind us.

"Nothing," Deets says, smiling.

"Nothing," says Darby, looking like she might cry.

Mrs. Larson decides to ignore them. I don't blame her. The bell already rang, and she probably wants to go do whatever teachers do on the weekend.

"Take good care of Riley, Lily," Mrs. Larson says. "Remember to feed him his healthy diet twice a day and *always* have water available. I know you will be responsible and do an excellent job, right? I'll see you both on Monday."

When we get to my house, we set up Riley's cage on the desk in my room and watch him for a while. I think it's his twitchy nose and his whiskers that make him SO cute.

"We should dress him up!" Darby says.

We go to the toy box and look for some doll clothes. We find Barbie shoes to put on him.

Riley's back feet are too big, but they fit on his front paws.

Darby lifts him by the shoes and stands him up. All of a sudden, his little paws slip out from the high heels and he takes off so fast, I have no chance of catching him! He runs down my bedspread onto the floor and out my door. We run after him. Too late.

"Mom!" I yell. "Riley got away!"

Yee-haw!

Mom runs downstairs carrying a plastic bowl and spends the next hour creeping around our house like a cat, ready to pounce.

"Got him!" she yells from Abby's room.

We run in. She's on the floor of Abby's closet with the bowl on the ground.

"Did you catch him?" I ask.

She lifts up the edge of the bowl and peeks under it, then starts cracking up. When she takes the bowl away, we see that she's just trapped one of Abby's dirty white tennis shoes! We all start laughing.

"I've been so jumpy," she says. "I mean, I want to find him, but I don't want to find him, if you know what I mean."

After that, Mom gives up and helps Dad with dinner.

"Maybe Riley swam to my end of the lake to hang out with the frogs," Darby says.

"It's not funny," I say. "I'm responsible for Riley. I can't lose him!"

Riley doesn't make an appearance until that night when we're all watching a movie and he scurries across the rec room floor.

Dad yells, "Get the mousetrap!"

"Dad! No!" I say. "That's our school rat!"

Before we go to bed, Darby and I put a plate of Riley's food near his cage. Mom suggests that we put some cheese out, but we don't want to mess up his diet. When we wake up, Riley's food is still there, and there's no sign of him except for some rat poop.

"What are we going to do?" I ask Darby. "I don't want to go to school on Monday and have to tell Mrs. Larson that we lost Riley."

Then we hear Abby yelling from her room.

"Lily!" she yells. "I found him!"

"It's probably the shoe," I say.

We open Abby's door and see Snort with her head stuck under Abby's bed, barking away. Abby is standing there in the middle of the floor, pointing. She looks like she's going to cry.

"Your stupid rat ate my candy collection!" she says.

We look under the bed, and Riley is there surrounded by shredded wrappers and nibbled-on candy bars. He's got chocolate all over his pink nose and white whiskers. I reach in and grab him. I guess he's too full of candy to try to run away.

"We ruined the experiment!" I say.

"You ruined my candy collection!" Abby says. "And I can't even tell Mom because she doesn't know I have one."

"Riley, you are a naughty rat," Darby says as we take him back to his cage.

"Now what are we going to do?" I ask her. "We ruined everything! What are we going to tell Mrs. Larson?"

"We don't really have to *tell* her," Darby says. "We don't really know what he ate anyway, so we can just make up a little story."

"But that's a lie," I say. "And we don't lie!"

"Don't worry," Darby says. "This isn't a real lie like Deets tells. It's not a *bad* lie; it's just a teeny-tiny lie."

Teeny-Tiny Lie

"It doesn't really count. Like when my brother tooted during his piano recital and asked me if I heard it, and I said no so he wouldn't freak out and make us miss going for ice cream afterward. So it's just like that. We're telling a story so no one has to worry. And I'm good at telling stories, so leave it to me."

Darby fills in the food chart with a perfect diet for the weekend for Riley. Then we cross our fingers that he doesn't gain weight before Monday.

Chapter 10

Darby's House

On Monday morning, the whole class gathers around to weigh the rats. Riley gained six grams over the weekend.

"What in the world did you feed him, Lily?" asks Mrs. Larson. "Candy bars?"

Mrs. Larson is smiling while she says it, and I can tell she's joking, but I turn bright red anyway.

"Um, I—I, uh . . ." I stammer.

"It must be all muscle!" Darby says. "I stayed over with Lily and I saw him. He didn't get off the exercise wheel all weekend!"

"Wow!" Mrs. Larson exclaims. "See what a difference exercise can make, children? What a sprightly, healthy rat!"

She nods at me in approval.

Darby winks at me.

I imagine a teeny-tiny lie on Darby's head. It looks happy that we aren't in trouble. *I'm* happy that we aren't in trouble! Maybe teeny-tiny lies aren't that bad. But if honesty is the best policy, aren't *all* lies bad?

For the rest of the day, I watch Riley. He's been lying on his back in his hammock, sleeping with his eyes open, which makes him look dead. I hope all the candy isn't going to kill him. Every time I have a chance, I go over and shake his cage a little to make sure he's still alive.

After school I go with Darby to her house, since Mom's at work. She's a dental hygienist

(which is why I don't have any cavities; well, that and the vegetables for snacks). As usual Mom arranged for me to go to Darby's and she didn't ask me first.

It's not that I don't like going to Darby's. I do. It's just that I kind of dread it, too. Her house is the oldest on the lake—more than a hundred years old. Darby says there are lots of ghosts from all the people who have died there. Now I know there are dead cows, too!

Darby and I get on her bus and find a seat. Darby's little sister, Katy, who's in second grade, sits down behind us.

"Can't you find another seat?" Darby asks Katy.

"*You* find another seat!" Katy says.

They stick their tongues out at each other. We pull away from the curb, and I immediately start thinking about the ghosts.

"I was so scared of your house the first time I came over," I tell Darby.

"I'm scared every day at my house!" Darby says.

"I used to be scared," says Katy. "But then I found out the ghosts are nice. They keep me company when I'm sleeping."

I shiver. The worst story Darby told me was the one about her parents' bedroom. She said that they were painting their room red, and a ghost walked through the paint and left footprints up the wall and across the ceiling. I was so scared to see her parents' room, but when she showed it to me, there were no footprints.

"They painted over them," Darby explained, like it was obvious.

That's the kind of thing that happens. Darby tells me about something haunted, but there's no *real* proof of it.

We get off the bus and run through an old metal gate and down Darby's driveway. She unlocks her creaky front door. No one is home. Her mom isn't back from work yet; her big brother, Kyle, who's in sixth grade, is at soccer; and her little brother, Deke, who's three, is at day care.

"Let's play on the computer," Darby says when we get inside.

We go to her parents' room. When we walk in, Darby gasps.

"What?" I say, afraid she sees a ghost.

"The pictures!" she says, pointing at the dresser.

"What pictures?"

"All the pictures of my mom and dad are gone from the dresser!"

"Where'd they go?"

"I don't know."

Darby looks like she's going to cry.

"Maybe my dad took them to put up in his cabin, so it's not so scary in there," she says. "That makes sense."

Darby's dad moved to a cabin on the lake not far away, so he could work on his ghost stories in peace and quiet. Mom said she's not sure that's the only reason he moved, but when I asked her what she meant, she wouldn't tell me.

"There's a picture under the dresser," I say, noticing the corner of a frame.

We look under the dresser and see lots of photos piled up. Darby starts putting them back on the dresser and on the walls.

"I can't get to the ones near the back," she says. "Let's pull the dresser out."

It's heavy, so I push on the back corner and Darby pulls on the front, until one side moves away from the wall. I can't *believe* what I see.

"Oh, yeah," Darby says. "My parents left them behind the furniture for proof that we have a ghost."

She looks at me. I must look as white as a ghost.

"What?" Darby asks. "Didn't you believe me?"

I didn't. But I do now. I want to leave Darby's parents' room.

"Let me get the rest of these pictures," Darby says, reaching behind the dresser like there aren't red ghost footprints on the wall.

She puts them back up and stares at them, looking sad.

"Are you okay?" I ask.

She kicks the dresser, stomps out of the room, sits down at the piano, and starts pounding the keys. Darby is super good at the piano, but right now she's making a bunch of loud sounds with her fists. Then she stops and acts like she's fine again. Weird.

"Let's go outside," she says.

We walk down her big grassy hill toward the lake. She gets some life jackets from a bucket inside a shed, and we go out to her dock.

"Let's catch frogs," she says.

We get on her pedal boat and pedal like we're on a bike. Darby is pedaling extra fast. I think she's still upset. We cut through the lily pads, looking down their long stems into the water to see if we can find any frogs' eggs. I find a frog swimming and pick it up.

We spend the next hour catching frogs. At my end of the lake, there is only a giant bullfrog, but this side of the lake is loaded with frogs. Once we have at least twenty, we pedal to the shore in the swamp and let them hop away into the mud.

Darby seems normal again after all the frog catching.

"Let's go visit the pigs!" she says. "I know how to get there through the blueberry farm."

We pedal the boat to shore in the swamp and tie it to a tree. Darby leads us along a path through a bunch of blueberry bushes to the pigsty.

"SOOO-EEEEY!" I yell, imitating Mom.

The three little piglets come running toward us. Darby and I open the gate, go into the sty, and pet them.

"I won't let you be food," I say to Bacon, kissing the spot on the top of his head. "You're too cute!"

We promise them that we will come again, then pedal back to Darby's house for dinner. It's loud now. Kyle is upstairs practicing his electric guitar, Katy is practicing the piano, and Deke is pounding on a pan with some spoons. He stops and looks at me.

Hi, Weewee!

Deke has a speech impediment. The worst part is that my sister, Abby, heard Deke call me Weewee, so now whenever she's mad at me, that's what she calls me, too.

We help set the table, then we sit down for dinner. All the kids start chanting and pounding their cups on the table. "Milk! Milk! Milk!"

"Get it yourself!" Darby's mom says, laughing. "What is this, a zoo?"

It is a zoo! The Dorski Zoo—and I actually kind of love it here.

"Let's go out and see Tootsie and Roll," Darby says after dinner.

She takes me to the garage where there's a big freezer and opens it up.

"You know what cow ghosts say?" Darby asks me. "MOOOOOOOO!"

I look in the freezer, and there are little wrapped packages. One is labeled "Roll Tongue" and another "Tootsie Flank."

Luckily Mom drives up.

Saved by the horn.

Chapter 11

The Big
BAD Lie

"Today we have a special guest," says a fifth-grade girl on SHTV the next morning.

"This is Ms. Meany," the co-anchor says. "She's our school counselor, and she's here to talk about bullying and healthy relationships."

"Hee-hee! Ms. *Meany*?" says Darby, laughing. "Talking about bullying?"

Everyone starts laughing.

"Children!" says Mrs. Larson. "Please listen!"

"Good morning, Sunny Hills students!" says Ms. Meany cheerily. "Today we will be discussing healthy relationships, with a focus on bullying. I've learned from our playground monitor, Mrs. 'Stache—Oh!'"

Ms. Meany turns red.

"I mean . . . Mrs. Rash," she continues. "Mrs. Rash has let me know that she has observed an increase in bullying on the playground. It's important that we all learn to identify a bully, and if we see bullying, that we stand up and stop it or report it to an adult."

I know why bullying has increased on the playground: Deets. He's making it cool to be mean.

"I'd like to show you a short video," Ms. Meany continues, "to help you learn to identify bullies and what to do about them."

Then she plays the *dumbest* animation of a bunch of farm animals bullying a spotted goat named Spotty. They tease Spotty for his spots, and he goes into a corner of the barn and cries— *MAAAAA, MAAAAA*—until a big bull named Baxter comes along and teaches everyone a lesson.

"Hey, farm animals!" says Baxter. "When you make fun of Spotty's coat, it makes him feel different and lonely. See how sad he is?"

Spotty turns around from his corner in the barn, and a tear drips from his eye.

"I'm sorry, Spotty," says a lamb. "I feel *ba-a-a-ad*."

"Cock-a-doodle, me too!" says a rooster. "I'm just jealous of your spotted coat because it's so pretty, but I was mean. I won't bully *anymore*!"

Then all the animals look at us.

The fifth-graders on SHTV clap along with Ms. Meany.

"Now, please," says Ms. Meany, "if you spot someone bullying on the playground, either try to stop it or report it to a trusted adult like myself or Mrs. 'Sta—Rash.'"

"Bye for now," say the fifth-graders. "Have a great rainy day at Sunny Hills!"

After SHTV, we measure and weigh the rats. The junk-food rats are starting to weigh more than the health-food Riley.

"Just like my junk-food dad is getting fatter than my health-food mom!" says José.

"José," says Mrs. Larson. "That's not necessary."

But I see her smile.

We record everything in our journals, then Mrs. Larson gives us time to clean our desks. We have to empty out the trays and throw away all of our garbage.

I'm busy cleaning my tray, when I hear Billy Snitch yell, "Teacher! Teacher!"

He's running to Mrs. Larson. I'm into organizing my supplies, so I don't pay much attention. Besides, Billy's always telling on somebody for something.

Then I hear Mrs. Larson say, "Lily, please come over here."

I look up. Darby is standing by Mrs. Larson's desk, crying and pointing at me.

I walk toward her. It's like a movie where some really ominous music starts playing, because I just know something bad is about to happen.

Mrs. Larson holds up Darby's crumpled drawing of the *David* statue—the one she shoved in the back of her desk. Poor Darby!

"Did you draw this?" Mrs. Larson asks me.

"Me? No!"

My drawing was much better than that! I think. *It had* contrapposto*!*

Darby's lip is quivering, and her nose is all red.

"Darby says that you drew this," Mrs. Larson says.

"I—I, uh," I say, looking at Darby, who's now crying so hard, her face is all scrunched up like a cartoon.

How to look INNOCENT by Lily

1. Tilt head down.
2. Look up.
3. Bat eyelashes.
4. Shrug.

Why is she blaming me?

Mrs. Larson looks from my face to Darby's. I'm trying to look innocent, but it seems like I'm making myself look guilty.

"Lily and Darby, this is the last straw," she finally says. "You need to understand that this is on a different level than the other drawings you have been in trouble for. *Those* drawings were disrespectful; *this* drawing is *completely* inappropriate for school, or anywhere, for that matter."

"Except Italy," Darby sniffles.

Mrs. Larson ignores her. It's definitely *not* clear that Darby's drawing is supposed to be Michelangelo's *David*.

"I will be calling your parents about this," she says.

My stomach does a flip.

"But Lily drew it. Why should I get in trouble?" Darby cries.

I look at her. I can't believe that she's lying to the teacher like this—about me—her best friend! This isn't a teeny-tiny lie. This is a Big Bad Lie! Mrs. Larson looks at me.

"Lily, I will ask you again. Did you draw this picture?"

I wait for Darby. *Say something!* But she doesn't. How am I supposed to blame Darby when she's standing here crying with snot all over her face? She looks so pitiful. Anyway, I did draw one, too; Darby's just the one who got caught.

"I . . . I did draw one, but . . ." I mumble.

"You did draw it?" Mrs. Larson says.

Mrs. Larson looks at both of us again. She *must* know that my drawing would be better than that. I nod my head up and down.

"You're sure you did this, Lily?" Mrs. Larson says.

I look at Darby again, but she just stares straight ahead.

I nod yes again because I don't know what else to do.

"Okay, Lily," Mrs. Larson says. "If you drew this, then I will put this in *your* file and have Principal Walker call your parents. But I expect *both* of you to make better choices from now on."

I walk to my desk. Darby sits at her desk but doesn't look at me. How could she blame me for that picture? Couldn't she have blamed Billy? He's the one who told on her.

After school I walk to the bus with Darby, since I'm going to her house today. Mom's working again, so I know I can't get out of it.

I sit down next to her. She's crying, facing the window. The bus lurches, and we ride along silently like that: me looking down at my backpack, Darby looking out the window.

"Darby," I say, "you *know* that was the picture *you* drew. I took mine home. I threw it away!"

How could she be like this? We both know that she drew the picture, but here she is telling me that *I* drew it.

"But you broke our Rizzlerunk pledge!" I say. "You're lying and being a bully, just like Deets!"

"I didn't draw it!" Darby says, squeezing her eyes shut, then starting to bawl all over again.

She's sobbing loudly, and people start looking at us.

"Forget it," I say.

When we get to her house, she acts like everything is normal. We make microwave popcorn and have chocolate milk, then build a fort in her bedroom. I try to act normal, too, but I can't stop thinking about what she did. She's my best friend, and she blamed me for something I didn't do—something really bad! And now *I'm* going to get in trouble.

When Mom picks me up, I can tell she already knows.

"Mr. Wilson called me," she says.

"He did?" I say, acting surprised.

"He told me that you drew a picture in class that was quite inappropriate."

"Inappropriate?" I ask, playing dumb because I don't know how much she knows.

Innapropri-what?

"As in *nude-drawing* inappropriate."

She knows everything. I can't hold it in anymore.

"Darby drew it!" I say. "And she told Mrs. Larson that I did it!"

"Lily Lattuga, don't lie to me," Mom says.

"I'm not! I *don't lie*! I swear! Darby drew the picture."

"Did you tell that to Mrs. Larson?"

"I didn't say that I drew it," I tell her, "but I didn't say that I *didn't* draw it, either. I felt too bad because Darby was crying so hard."

"So you took the blame to protect Darby?" Mom asks.

"I guess so," I say. "Is that good?"

"Did it make you feel better?" Mom asks.

"No, it just got me in trouble," I say. "And I'm really mad at Darby."

"Should I call Principal Walker and explain the situation?" Mom asks me.

"I don't know," I say. "I feel bad getting Darby in trouble. She's been acting weird anyway."

"She does have a lot going on," Mom says. "But that doesn't mean she should blame you for this. It's up to you to decide whether you'll suffer the consequences for Darby's decision."

"What consequences?"

"The RTC for three days," says Mom.

My heart stops and drops into my shoes.

Thunk

Chapter 12
Loyalty and Honesty

The next morning at school, I see Darby in the coatroom.

"Hi, Lily Pad!" she says.

I look at her smiling at me. Isn't she going to say anything? Like *Thanks for taking the blame for the drawing*? I thought at least she'd thank me. I thought she'd treat me like her hero—but instead she's pretending like it never even happened!

"Darby, I have to go to the RTC for the next three days for the drawing *you* did!" I blurt out, almost crying.

"I didn't do it," Darby says. "It wasn't my drawing. I thought it was yours."

"That's impossible, Darby! It was in *your* desk. I took my drawing home and threw it away."

"I didn't do it!" she says, squeezing her eyes shut just like she did yesterday.

Then she turns around, walks into class, and sits down. I don't understand why she's being like this. She's *lying* to me!

I sit at my desk. Deets kicks her a few times like he does every day, big bully.

"Stop it!" Darby says. "I didn't do it!"

"Do what?" says Deets.

"Nothing."

She looks angry and pounds her fists on the desk like she did on her piano. Even though there's no sound, I can hear the angry chords.

"Darby, what's wrong with you?" I ask her.

"Nothing," she says.

After we take roll and watch SHTV, Mrs. Larson fills us in on another nutrition project.

She has an empty pie chart that we are supposed to fill in with the proper foods that should be eaten every day.

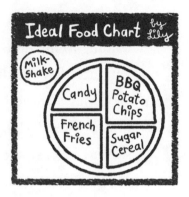

"Who can guess what food group goes here in this slice of the plate?" asks Mrs. Larson, pointing to one of the two biggest slices.

"Pie!" shouts David. "Lemon meringue pie!"

Mrs. Larson raises her eyebrow at him.

"It must be vegetables," Mikey says. "Because if it's the biggest, it would have to be the least fun to eat."

"Correct," says Mrs. Larson, writing *vegetables* in the lower left slice. "But actually, vegetables can be quite tasty!"

She sounds like Mom.

"It's true!" Darby says. "I eat raw vegetables at Lily's house all the time, because that's the only food they ever have. I dip them in hummus, which is delicious. Hummus is yummus!"

I look at Darby and I feel sad. I *like* Darby coming to my house. But how can I stay friends with her after she did this to me?

"Does anyone have a guess as to what goes in this slice?" Mrs. Larson asks, pointing to the second biggest slice. I know it's grains because Mom showed me at home. I raise my hand.

"Grains?" I say—or ask, in case I'm wrong, which is a trick for answering questions if you're supershy.

"Yes!" says Mrs. Larson. "Grains. But not just any grains—*whole* grains."

"Like, one time I ate a *whole loaf* of bread!" says Sonja Lee.

"Well, that's not really what I mean, Sonja," says Mrs. Larson.

We fill in the other slices: fruits and protein and a serving of dairy or dairy alternative (preferably a milkshake, in my opinion).

"Our homework for this week," says Mrs. Larson as she passes out sheets of paper with the food chart on the top and a blank plate at the bottom, "will be to plan and cook a well-balanced meal for your family. We should all be eating as healthfully as our healthy rat!"

After we fill in our plans, David shares first.

"I'm making ketchup with French fries, special sauce with cheeseburgers, and ranch dressing with salad," he says.

Ketchup with French Fries

Billy is making sushi, which everyone thinks is amazing, of course, but Mrs. Larson looks worried and tells him to make sure he gets very fresh fish.

"I'm making sushi, too," Deets says, "and I don't have to worry, because my dad makes sushi, and he says we get the best fish you can buy—straight from Japan."

"Of course you do," Mrs. Larson says, and I swear she rolls her eyes.

"I'm going to make chili and corn bread," I say when Mrs. Larson calls on me.

"Chili rhymes with Lily!" Darby says, smiling at me.

I can't look at her.

"I'm making vegetarian lasagna!" says Iris.

Sonja is making enchiladas, and Gabriella is making spaghetti and meatballs. Ethan is the only one who has to do his whole meal plan over because all he's written on his planner is "Happy Meal."

At recess, Darby wants to go to our invisible clubhouse like nothing is wrong.

"I'm going to the library," I say.

"Lily, I told you that it wasn't my picture! That drawing was yours."

"It was not, Darby! Mine was way better," I say, turning on my heels toward the library. "I don't understand why you're lying about this. Loyalty and honesty for all. It's our Rizzlerunk pledge! How can you break it? I would *never* lie to you."

"I didn't lie!" Darby insists, shutting her eyes in that weird way again.

"Just because you say something is true doesn't make it true," I say.

Darby looks like she might start crying, but I'm so mad I don't care. I spin around and walk to the library, which is the best place to go when you're not having a good day, because you can always find a story and go somewhere else in your imagination. Iris is in the beanbag where she usually sits. She's reading a new thick book with a picture of a brain on the front.

"Hi, Lily," she says. "Want to sit with me? I can share the beanbag."

"Sure," I say. "What are you reading?"

"It's a story about a girl who can read people's minds."

"Really? I wish I could read minds."

"Why?" asks Iris.

"Well, Darby lied about something, and I know she lied—but she won't tell me the truth. She got me in trouble."

"Oh," Iris says. "Sorry about that. But would you *really* want to read someone's mind?"

"I just said I would," I say. "Wouldn't you?"

She sits and stares for a moment. She looks like she sees a fly on the wall, but I think she's thinking.

"Not really," she says. "If you could read someone's mind, you'd know everything they were thinking. Would you really want to know *everything* someone is thinking? Like today, when I said I was making vegetarian lasagna, I'll bet everyone thought it was weird. But I don't really *know* that. What if I could read everyone's minds and hear them thinking *weirdo, weirdo.* I might never come back to school."

"Well," I say, "you'd also have heard me thinking it was cool."

"Really?" she asks.

"Yeah," I say. "We just got a new piglet, and my parents are going to kill it, and we are going to eat it, so now I want to be a vegetarian like you. So, see, not everyone thought it was weird."

"I guess I would've liked to have read your mind," she says.

"I thought you didn't care what people think of you," I say. "At least it seems like that."

"I don't really," she says, "but I'm still glad I don't know *exactly* what they think."

"What if we could read Deets Frizzle's mind?" I say.

"That's funny," Iris says. "He seems very imaginative with all his made-up stuff. I kind of feel sorry for him, though. Did you notice that no one is really *nice* to him? I mean, they act like he's cool and hang out with him, but no one really *likes* him."

"I never thought of that, but I guess so," I say. "Plus, I think his dad, or maybe his uncle, is mean to him, too. Darby and I saw it. But he's such a liar, it's hard to feel sorry for him."

"I know," says Iris. "Everyone wants a pet tiger cub, of course, but just because you say something is true doesn't make it true."

"That's what I said to Darby!"

"So what did Darby blame you for?" she asks me.

"Oh," I say, feeling myself turning red. "She drew an inappropriate picture, and Billy Snitch grabbed it and told on her. Next thing I knew, she was telling Mrs. Larson that I did it! Then she started bawling and I felt bad, so I didn't tell Mrs. Larson it was hers."

"Hmm," Iris says. "I guess Darby didn't want to get into trouble. Especially right now."

"What do you mean, especially right now?"

"Her parents are getting divorced," she says. "Didn't you know?"

"No," I say, wondering why Darby didn't tell me. "How do you know? Are you sure?"

"My mom is friends with Darby's mom," she says. "She told me. She said Darby already knows, but she asked me not to tell anyone. Oops."

The bell rings.

"Thanks for letting me hang out with you, Iris," I say. "You should be part of the Rizzlerunk Club with us. Well . . . if we still have a club."

"You should stay friends with Darby," she says. "She's nice. It'll be okay."

Chapter 13
The RTC

During free time, I have to go for my first day at the RTC. I look at Darby on my way out the door, and she stares at her feet, like she's never seen her shoes before. Then Deets gets up, too. Oh, great, I have to go to the RTC with Deets Frizzle. I heard that he'd pushed Ethan from behind on the balance bar and knocked him down into the wood chips, but I didn't know we'd have to go to the RTC together.

"This school is stupid," Deets says to me. "Mrs. 'Stache said I was bullying just because I pushed Ethan down at recess the other day, but he said he was stronger than me and that's not true! I'm stronger than everyone. I'm stronger than my brother and my dad put together!"

Maybe you're stronger than your little shih tzu, I think, but keep it to myself. If that was Deets's dad we saw, there's no way Deets is stronger. He's probably not even meaner. Deets's dad looked like he would beat up anyone, including the shih tzu.

"I heard you pushed Ethan off the balance bar from behind," I say.

"Did not! I punched him right in the chest, and he fell 'cause I'm the strongest kid at this whole dumb school."

"Were you the strongest kid at your old school?" I ask him, knowing what he'll say.

"Of course I was, and everyone knew it!"

"Why do you lie about everything?" I ask Deets.

"I don't lie about anything," Deets says. "I'm as honest as George Washington."

"That's a *lie*!" I say. "I don't get why people have to lie about stuff. I don't lie. I never lie."

"Never?" says Deets. "You've *never* lied."

"Never," I say. "And I *won't* lie. Ever."

"That's a lie," Deets says.

We walk quietly for a minute.

"S-s-o," Deets stammers. "Why is this place called the Raccoon Training Center? Are there really rabid raccoons in there? Will they do electric shock therapy on us?"

I smile because the rumors about the RTC have gotten even worse—and Deets sounds scared! I want to tell him it's true what he's heard—maybe I could even make it sound much, much worse— but unlike Darby and Deets, *I won't lie.*

"That's a good one," I say. "I haven't heard about the raccoons before. Who told you that?"

"Darby," he says.

"Well, Darby's a liar," I say. "The RTC isn't fun, but it's not *that* bad. You just have to sit there and write about why you did what you did until recess is over. It's just you have to do it with Mrs. 'Stache there."

Mrs. 'Stache is standing by the door of the RTC room.

"Deets Frizzle," she says. "Big man on the playground. I knew from the moment I saw you that I'd be seeing you in the RTC."

Deets freezes.

"Don't just stand there! Sit!" Mrs. 'Stache commands, pointing to a seat in the front of the classroom.

Deets sits. Then I swear he starts to cry, but I don't want to stare. I think of how scared he looked that day I saw him in the driveway, and I want to tell Mrs. 'Stache not to be so mean to him, but I don't want to get into even more trouble.

I'm not sure what to do, so I stand and wait. When I look at Mrs. 'Stache, I give her a little smile, because last time I was in here, Mrs. 'Stache was actually kind of nice in her comments on my writing. I found out from her notes that she's an artist, and since I'm an artist, too, I thought maybe she'd like me more this time.

"Lily Lattuga," she says, squinting. "You've gone a whole month without being in here. Congratulations. This is your second visit. Three strikes you're out, you know. No doubt you'll hit a home run in no time with *your* bad behavior."

"It wasn't my drawing," I mumble.

"What did you say?" says Mrs. 'Stache.

"It wasn't my drawing!" I say.

It feels good to say it out loud.

"Sure it wasn't," says Mrs. 'Stache.

"But, it wasn't! I *did* do a drawing of Michelangelo's *David*, but I took it home," I say. "I know it wasn't mine, because mine was better. My drawing *looked* like the *David* statue. And it had *contrapposto*! You couldn't tell Darby's drawing was the *David* at all."

Mrs. 'Stache looks surprised, maybe even impressed! Since she is also an artist, I was hoping the word *contrapposto* would have this effect.

It doesn't last.

"Sit!" she commands, pointing to a seat in the back far corner.

I sit.

Mrs. 'Stache explains what we have to do, which is spend recess writing about why we shouldn't have done what we did. Deets wipes his eyes, and we both write until the bell rings. We give Mrs. 'Stache our papers on the way out the door.

RETURN to the RTÖ

Help me!

to the RTÖ by Lily

DAY 1

Dear Mrs. Rash,
I am sorry (again) for causing a problem
at school, even though I didn't do it!
Like I said, my drawing was WAY
better than Darby's.

← Contrapposto Cat
(Fully dressed!)

Lily, I didn't learn
about contrapposto
until art school.
Nice execution.
-Mrs. R

   I guess it's fair that I'm here
anyway, but it's NOT FAIR because I'm
not the one who got caught.
DARBY WAS! And Darby got caught
because stupid Billy Snitch is the
biggest tattletale in the universe.
   Why did Darby blame me? I didn't
tell on her because I didn't want to
get my best friend (ex-best friend)
in trouble, and she has stuff going
on that Iris told me about, but I'm
not supposed to know. I can't
say what it is here.
   Mrs. Rash, please don't show this
to Mrs. Larson. I don't want to

Next page ➤

get Darby in trouble. All I want is for her to tell me the TRUTH so we can go back to being best friends under frogs, with loyalty and honesty for all. Except how can I trust her anymore ??????

This is my new pig, Bacon!!

I'm so cute!

I'm going to save him from being bacon. Darby was going to help, but I guess now I'll do it myself. Iris says Darby is nice and I should stay friends with her. But FRIENDS DON'T LIE!

FRIENDS DON'T LIE!

FRIENDS DON'T LIE!

Lily,
Good friends are hard to come by. Trust me. Everyone makes mistakes. Let me know if your parents have too much pork. I will buy some.
—Mrs. Rash
P.S. I, too, like drawing. Alas, mainly on my shopping lists.

Sincerely,
Lily Lattuga

P.S. Sorry for the drawings. I remember last time you LIKED THEM !!!

P.P.S. There goes the bell. YAY!

Chapter 14
Chefs for a Night

When the weekend arrives, I wake up early, excited to do my nutrition assignment and cook for my family. I go upstairs. I can't believe it!

Pancakes for breakfast!

Abby already has a stack of pancakes on her plate, smeared with butter and drenched in syrup. She shovels a big bite into her mouth.

"Yuck!" she says, sticking out her tongue. "What did you put in the pancakes this time, Mom? I don't like them at all!"

"Oh, shoot," says Mom. "I made them with quinoa flour instead of regular flour. I was hoping you wouldn't notice."

Then Mom takes a bite.

"I admit, the flavor is a little strong," she says.

"Can't you just make normal pancakes like a normal mom?" I ask.

Dad eats his stack and mine.

"I heard you're making chili tonight, Lily," Dad says. "After breakfast, I'll take you to the store so we can buy the ingredients."

I love when Dad takes me shopping, because if I ask Dad for stuff like the junk-food rats eat, I know he'll buy it because he wants it, too.

Dad helps me find a good chili recipe on the Internet, but it has pork and beef in it.

"No animals!" I say.

So he finds a vegetarian chili recipe instead. We print it out and go to the store. We get all the ingredients, plus a box of Lucky Charms cereal, which Dad and I think is the best.

When we get home, Mom helps me cut up the green peppers and onions. The onions make us both start crying. Mom tells me that if you put a spoon in your mouth, upside down on your tongue, you won't cry as much, but I don't think it works.

After we're done with all the chopping, Mom leaves to work on her computer and I do the rest.

The chili recipe is kind of hard to follow, because whoever wrote it wasn't very good at capitalization.

```
1 T olive oil
2 t salt
2 T ground cumin
2 T tomato paste
5 t chili powder
```

Then I start the corn bread. I melt butter in the microwave, and it overflows. I crack an egg into the flour, then add hot butter and accidentally scramble the eggs. I mix it, pour it in a glass dish, and put it in the oven.

Then I set the table. Knife points to the fork? I don't know. I can never remember which side the knife and fork go on, and I know the only one who cares is Mom, so I just set it how I think looks good. I even put swan napkins on the plates.

When the timer rings, I call everyone up for dinner. We all sit down. I cut the corn bread, but it won't come off the bottom of the baking pan, so instead of slices, I serve piles of crumbs.

Dad takes the first bite of chili.

"Wooo wee!" he says. "I haven't had chili like this since we lived in Texas!"

Dad's eyes are watering, and he takes a big gulp of water.

"Ow! Ow! Ow!" Abby says, reaching for her milk. "Mommy! My mouth! My mouth is burning up!"

Mom takes a bite and starts fanning her mouth.

"How much chili powder did you put in here, Lily?"

"Just what the recipe said."

I take a bite and just about burn my tongue off, it's so spicy. I gulp my milk, but it doesn't help, so I take a bite of corn bread.

"Yuck!" I say.

"Oh, Lily," Mom says. "Too much baking soda in the corn bread! Did you follow the recipe?"

Suddenly I remember the *t* and *T*. I thought someone messed up typing the recipe but now I remember that a lowercase *t* means teaspoon and an uppercase *T* means tablespoon. I did tablespoons for everything! Five *tablespoons* of chili powder in the chili and two *tablespoons* of baking soda in the corn bread. No wonder it tastes all wrong.

"Dang!" I say. "I'm going to get an F."

"You get an A for effort," says Mom.

"Lucky Charms, anyone?" asks Dad.

"Yay!" Abby and I cheer.

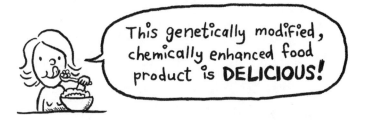

This genetically modified, chemically enhanced food product is **DELICIOUS!**

So we all have Lucky Charms for dinner. Even Mom.

"Well, how did the cooking go for everyone?" Mrs. Larson asks us on Monday morning.

David goes first.

"My ketchup turned out really good," he says, "since there was only one ingredient, which was ketchup. I burned my French fries in the oven, because I turned it on to five hundred and fifty degrees so I could get the fries to cook faster. So we had ketchup and potato chips instead. It's a really good combination! You should try it!"

"That's a good lesson, David," Mrs. Larson says. "Cooking isn't an easy thing to do. It takes practice. But sometimes chefs do learn from their mistakes."

Darby goes next.

"My chicken stir-fry stuck to the bottom of the wok," she tells us, "and my mom said eating the chicken was like chewing on erasers, so we went out to McDonald's!"

"My dog ate all the sushi," Billy says. "Then he threw up all night, so it was lucky he ate it and we didn't."

"My dad said my sushi was just as good as the sushi he makes," Deets says. "And even better than the sushi we ate in Japan."

It turns out that half the class ended up either eating breakfast for dinner or going out for fast food.

"Well, not all experiments turn out quite as planned," says Mrs. Larson. "Perhaps I should send a letter of apology to your parents! On another note, I have some news to share with you. I was watching the rats this morning, and I have a hunch that Ratsinburger and Marshmallow aren't doing as well as Riley. I think we're going to start seeing results that will prove our hypothesis about healthy food choices."

We all go over and look at the rats. Ratsinburger and Marshmallow are just hanging out at the bottom of the cage, sniffing and blinking. Riley is going full speed ahead on his wheel like a gym rat. Now the junk-food rats weigh *less* than Riley, because they aren't getting enough nutrition! Poor guys. I should sneak them my lunch.

Chapter 15
Rizzlerunks Forever

At recess, Darby wants to act like everything is normal.

"C'mon, best bud, let's go to the clubhouse," she says as we walk outside.

"I'm going to the library," I say, turning the other way.

"No," Darby says, grabbing my hand. "Invisible clubhouse! We haven't had a meeting in, like, a week."

"I'm not a Rizzlerunk anymore," I say. "You broke the pledge."

"I already told you," she says. "I didn't lie!"

I look at her. Maybe if we go to our clubhouse and say our pledge about loyalty and honesty and stuff, she'll feel bad and tell me the truth.

"Fine," I say. "I'll go."

We sit in the dirt like we always do. It feels normal. I like normal. We say our pledge, *with loyalty and honesty for all*. She looks me right in the eyes when she says it, but I see her hand go behind her back and I wonder if she's crossing her fingers.

"Darby, do you really think that was my drawing? The one you drew?"

"It wasn't mine!" she says. "Can we stop talking about it already?"

"It *was* yours! Darby, be honest."

"I am honest!" she says. "I'm the most honest one in my whole dumb family."

"What does this have to do with your family?" I ask her. "I'm talking about the picture."

"I didn't do it," she says, squeezing her eyes shut. "And that's that."

I'm so confused! It's impossible that she doesn't know that the drawing *she* drew was her drawing.

"Can we just talk about something else?" she says, opening her eyes wide. "Like Bacon!"

"I don't want to talk about bacon," I say. "I'm not eating bacon anymore."

"I know!" she says. "I mean, let's talk about your pig, Bacon! I've been thinking about our rescue."

"You have?" I ask.

"Yeah. Look. This is Bacon's sty," she says, drawing a square in the dirt. Then she draws another square and connects them with a line. "And these are the woods by my house where we can let Bacon go."

She walks her fingers down the path.

"When we see him, we can grab him and stuff him in a pillowcase. Then, if there's still room, we can get the other piggies, too. We could save all of them!"

"I'd like that," I say, picturing Bacon's cute little piglet face.

"They'll have plenty of bugs and pinecones and leaves and stuff to live on," says Darby. "They'll be so happy, they'll be snorting all over the forest!"

She starts snorting loudly.

"Darby, you're going to make your nose bleed!"

"No, I won't," she says. "It's fun. You should try it!"

Next thing I know, both Darby and I are rolling in the dirt, snorting like pigs. We don't notice the feet gathering around our clubhouse.

"Ha ha!" says Gabriella. "They really are pigs!"

"Dirty pigs, rolling in the dirt!" says Sonja.

"Dumb pigs!" Tillie says.

"Good one, Tillie," says Darby. "Super creative!"

Darby has a talent for sarcasm, too.

"I'm gonna catch you and turn you into bacon if you don't stop snorting like that," Deets says.

Darby snorts at him.

"Let's get 'em!" yells Deets.

Darby and I jump up and run like pigs from a butcher. We have at least fifteen people following us. I look down and see that Darby's shoe is untied.

"Darby! Your shoe!"

Too late. She trips. She would have fallen face-first right into the concrete, but instead she falls right into a cushion—Mrs. 'Stache's tummy.

"You two again," Mrs. 'Stache says, recovering her breath. "Surprise, surprise."

"Everyone was chasing us!" Darby says. "They were bullying us!"

I look back, but now the playground is empty. Somehow the bell rang, and everyone ran back to class.

"Bullying, ha!" Mrs. 'Stache says. "Trying to double your time in the RTC, Lily?"

"No!" I say. "We just didn't hear the bell."

"It wasn't Lily's fault, Mrs. Rash," Darby says. "I'm the one who started snorting like a pig, so everyone was teasing us and chasing us. If you're going to get mad at us for being chased by bullies, I'm the one who should get into trouble."

I look at Darby with my mouth open. Now she's taking the blame for something? She's saving me!

"That's perfect, Dorski," says Mrs. 'Stache. "You running around snorting with your shoe untied like a slovenly pig."

"Pigs are actually clean," Darby says.

Mrs. 'Stache glares at her.

"TIE YOUR SHOE!" she yells.

Darby bends down and ties her shoe. I notice her hands are shaking. She's scared.

"I was snorting, too, Mrs. Rash," I blurt out.

"Of course you were," she says. "I wouldn't expect any less of you."

"Mrs. Rash," says Darby. "They were *bullying* us! We're supposed to tell you if we are getting bullied."

Mrs. 'Stache squints at both of us.

"GET BACK TO CLASS!" she yells.

Darby and I sprint to class.

"Mrs. 'Stache is the biggest bully of all!" Darby says.

I look at Darby. She was going to take the blame for me. She *is* nice, just like Iris said. Most people are still in the coatroom when we get back to class, so we sneak in without Mrs. Larson noticing we're late.

When Darby sits down, Deets looks at her and snorts.

"Pig Whisperer," he says.

"Yep," says Darby. "Rat Whisperer *and* Pig Whisperer! Maybe I'll be a vet when I grow up."

"I'd be a better veterinarian than you," says Deets.

"Deets Frizzle, you are a the biggest liar on the planet," says Darby.

"Teacher!" says Billy. "Darby is bullying Deets."

"Thank you for your report, Billy. I think Deets will be just fine," she says.

I like Mrs. Larson even more because I can tell she likes Deets about as much as Darby and I do.

Dr. Darby Dolittle

The BEST Vet!

Chapter 16
Honesty Is the Best Policy

"Today we have a special guest in class," says Mrs. Larson. "This is Ms. Meany, our school counselor. You all saw her on SHTV last week discussing bullying. She's here to talk about healthy relationships again. This time, she will be focusing on honesty."

"Hello, Mrs. Larson's class!" says Ms. Meany. "Today we will be splitting into groups and working together to fill out a worksheet about honesty. But first, let's discuss honesty. What *is* honesty?"

Sonja raises her hand.

"It's when you don't lie to your best friend about having a sleepover with your other best friend without you," she says, looking right at Gabriella.

Gabriella and Tillie smile at each other. I guess the Gabbys lie to each other, too. But that doesn't mean Darby and I should be like them.

"Honesty," says Mikey, looking at Sonja, "is when you *don't* tell your friend that I *like* like her, when I don't."

Sonja looks at Gabriella, who frowns. I see Darby smile, and I know what she's thinking, which is that if Mikey doesn't like Gabriella, maybe he likes her!

"Honesty is when you don't make up stories," Darby says, looking at Deets, "like how you'd be a better veterinarian than me, or that you have a pet shark, or live in the newest house on Pine Lake, when you don't even *live* on Pine Lake at all."

"Not true!" says Deets.

"Ahem." Ms. Meany clears her throat. "These are all good examples of *how* to be honest, but first I'd like to *define* honesty."

Iris raises her hand.

"Honesty is when you tell the truth," she says.

"Well put, Iris," says Ms. Meany. "People who are honest often go down in history. Can anyone name an honest person in history?"

"George Washington 'cause of the cherry tree," shouts David.

"Yes," says Ms. Meany. "Correct. And can anyone name another president known for his honesty?"

"Abe Lincoln!" says Sonja.

"That's right. Abraham Lincoln was known as Honest Abe," Ms. Meany says.

"That's 'cause when Abraham Lincoln was working at his job at a store," says Sonja, "he accidentally counted someone's change wrong by a few cents, then he walked and walked and walked just to give back the money."

"That's right, Sonja," says Ms. Meany. "And another time, he was weighing out tea for a woman and accidentally gave her too little tea for her money. Guess what he did?"

"He walked and walked and walked," says José, "so he could bring her the tea."

"Correct," says Ms. Meany. "This was more than one hundred years ago, but we still know about it today. Truly, as George Washington said, honesty is . . ."

"The best policy!" we all finish her sentence.

"On the worksheet I'm handing out," Ms. Meany continues, "there will be several stories in which people make choices about honesty. I'd like you to pick the answer that you think is appropriate and explain your choice."

Mrs. Larson divides us into groups. I'm with Gabriella, Deets, Iris, Darby, and Mikey. Gabriella grabs the worksheet and starts reading.

"Question one," she says. "Tommy breaks his sister's fishbowl. His parents ask him if he broke it. If he did, he will face consequences. Which is an honest answer? (A) Tommy blames his sister for breaking the fishbowl. (B) Tommy admits to breaking the fishbowl. (C) Tommy tells his parents that a cat came through the window and broke the fishbowl."

"B," says Iris. "Obviously!"

"But he's going to be punished," says Deets. "I would say a cat did it because no one could ever prove that it didn't."

"But that's not the *right* answer," says Gabriella. She circles B.

"Okay," she says, "now we have to explain why Tommy would choose to tell the truth and get into trouble instead of lying."

"Because he'd feel bad if he lied," says Mikey.

"I wouldn't feel bad," says Deets. "I'd feel bad if I got into trouble. This way, no one gets in trouble except the cat—and there isn't even a cat!"

"He'd feel bad because it's not *okay* to lie," I say, glancing at Darby.

Nothing fishy here. Cat's honor!

"Right," says Iris. "He'd probably feel guilty."

"Yeah," says Mikey. "Plus, if he lies and his parents find out, they won't trust him."

"You guys are stupid," says Deets. "He'd get out of trouble if he lied, so he should lie. It doesn't hurt anyone."

"Except Tommy," says Darby.

I look at her. Does she feel bad about lying to me? It doesn't seem like it. If she did feel bad, wouldn't she have just admitted it by now?

Gabriella writes:

Tommy should tell the truth because he will always know he lied and will feel bad about it.

"Question two," says Gabriella. "Suzy borrowed her friend Amelia's favorite stuffed animal without asking and lost it. Amelia is looking for it. What should Suzy do? (A) Act as if she doesn't know what happened. (B) Surprise her friend with a new stuffed animal. (C) Admit to her friend that she borrowed the stuffed animal and lost it."

"She should admit it," I say. "Because honesty is the best policy."

"I wouldn't admit it," says Gabriella. "My friend would be mad at me, and I don't like when my friends are mad at me. I would just get her a new stuffed animal and say that I'm sorry she lost her old one. But, obviously, that's not the right answer."

"The right answer," says Deets, "is for her to act like she doesn't know what happened. That way her friend won't be mad at her. Easy."

"Wouldn't you feel bad about lying to your friend?" Iris says.

"No!" says Deets. "Why should I?"

"Because it's wrong!" I say.

Why is this so hard for some people to understand?

Gabriella writes:

Suzy could say her friend's sister took the stuffie and call her friend a liar. Nothing would happen, but it's not right.

After Ms. Meany leaves, Deets and I have to go to the RTC for the second time. We walk to the classroom, past Mrs. 'Stache, and immediately sit down and start writing so she doesn't yell at us.

RTC DAY 2

Hi, Mrs. Rash, it's Lily). I'm sorry again that I'm here in the RTC, even though I really shouldn't be here because I didn't do anything wrong. But, oh well. Here I am, so I apologize. My dad calls it a blanket apology because it covers everything. Like the bad stuff I did with Jill, it was not ~~nessesary~~ ~~necesary~~ nesessary(?) Writing helps me think. Maybe you're too busy monitoring the playground to think. Probably. You have a hard job, especially when it's raining.

Thinking Thing ↓

Lily, rain inspires artists the world over! — Mrs. R.

(like every day!)

Even though Darby and I are hanging out again, I still want her to tell me the **TRUTH** about that drawing. But, how? Hmm... idea!

I COULD TORTURE HER!

evil laugh → HA HA HA HA HA HA HA

Torture ideas:

① Tickle her feet! NOPE! Stinky feet. Too gross!

② Pinch her toes. <u>NO</u>... the stinky feet!

③ Pin her down. Hang spit over her face. Threaten to drop it. Nope. Won't work!

| Works on Abby | Darby TOO STRONG!! |

Flip

Nice try, weakling!

by Lily

HEY! I'VE GOT IT! TRUTH OR DARE!

idea!

It'll be SO FUN!!!

Darby will be too scared to do truth, so I could make her do lots of **DARES!** If I make the dares HORRIBLE enough, she'll have to tell me the **TRUTH!**

P.S. I know I'm not supposed to draw. Do you like my drawings, though?
— Lily

136

Chapter 17

Double Dare

After school, Darby invites me over, and I decide to go. (Maybe I can get this truth-or-dare game going!)

We get on the bus, and I look out the window and see Deets with that same man from his driveway. The man is holding Deets by the arm and walking so quickly that Deets can hardly keep up. I can tell he's doing one of those squeeze-holds parents do when a kid is in trouble. It looks like it hurts. Up close, the man is just like a bigger version of Deets. It has to be his dad.

"Deets's dad looks so mean!" I say to Darby.

"Yeah, it sucks when parents are mean," Darby says. "Even when they're not mean to the kids and they're just mean to each other."

My parents get grumpy sometimes, but they aren't mean to each other. It wouldn't be very fun if they were. I wonder if Darby is talking about her parents. Maybe they really are getting divorced, like Iris said. I'm about to ask when the bus stops.

"We're here!" Darby says.

"But this isn't your stop," I say.

"Yes, it is; it's my dad's cabin!"

"The haunted cabin?" I ask her. "Is your dad there?"

Darby's dad, Doug, lives in his cabin, where he's working on his book about real-life ghost stories. Last time we went there, he played a trick on us and scared us so bad, I almost peed my pants. His cabin is old, tiny, creaky, and scary.

"He's not there right now, but he'll be home soon," she tells me. "He said to help ourselves to snacks and make ourselves at home."

"At home?" I say. "It's too scary to feel at home!"

We walk through the thick pine trees down a long dirt road, splashing in mud puddles along the way. Something scurries through the bushes, and Darby and I both jump. Then we notice a cute little raccoon face peeking out at us.

"My dad feeds the raccoons raw eggs, so they come over and keep him company," Darby says. "There's a whole family of them."

"They're so cute," I say.

"Yeah, but vicious," says Darby. "And rats are cuter, in my opinion."

We get to the front door. I've only come from the lake and through the back door, so I haven't seen the front door before. I stop dead.

Darby explains, "It was the same ghost that walked on the walls in my parents' room."

Talk about creepy. She grabs my now-sweaty hand and pulls me inside. It looks just the same as it did the last time we were here. A small desk sits in the middle of the room, and on top of it is Doug's old-fashioned typewriter. There's paper in the typewriter. Darby and I read it.

The woman stood in her nightgown on the landing. The third stair creaked; it always creaked, she thought. But, when the toothless old man's foot had hit the step, it was silent. It's him. The ghost of her bedtime stories, the one she'd feared since she was a young girl. She screamed. The man began to laugh, a deep, cackling

"I'm glad that I've met your dad and he's so nice," I tell Darby. "Otherwise, I'd be out of here!"

Darby opens a cabinet, gets out some popcorn, and puts it into the microwave. The sound of popping makes me feel a little less scared.

While the popcorn pops, I call Mom and tell her where I am. Darby's dad has one of those old-fashioned phones with a dial, so Darby has to show me how to use it.

Huh?

She dumps the popcorn into a bowl, pours us some soda, and we sit down at the small kitchen table and eat.

"Want to play truth or dare?" I ask her, chomping on a kernel (which Mom and Dad told me not to do because I might break a tooth).

"Sure!" she says.

"Okay!" I say. "Me first. Truth or dare?"

"Hmm . . . dare," she says.

I knew she'd say that.

"I dare you to drink your whole soda at once."

"'K," she says, smiling. "Easy!"

She gulps and gulps and gulps, then sets down her cup and lets out a long burp.

"How'd you do that?" I ask her. "I can drink milk like that, but not bubbly soda!"

"Practice," she says. "Your turn. Truth or dare?"

"Truth," I say.

I have nothing to hide.

"Do you have a crush on anyone in our class?"

"What do you think?" I say.

"You have a crush on Deets."

"Nuh-uh!" I say. "I would never, ever, ever have a crush on Deets Frizzle! But I have a crush on Mikey, just like everyone else."

My face gets red and hot, like a bowl of tomato soup.

"He's mine, though," says Darby, popping a piece of popcorn into her mouth.

"Fine," I say. "Truth or dare?"

"Dare," she says.

I think my game is going to work!

"I dare you to go down to the lake and dip your whole head into the water."

"Okay," she says.

"It's gonna be cold!" I say.

I follow her out the door onto the slippery, creaky deck, and we cut our way through the long grass and bushes to the edge of the lake.

"Time for a dunk!" I say.

We walk a little way out onto the dock, and Darby lies on her back, takes off her glasses, and dunks her whole head into the water.

"Did it!" she says.

She's dripping water all over her clothes.

"Brr!" She shivers.

We go back into the cabin and get a towel from the bathroom. Darby dries her hair, then drapes the towel around her like a cloak. The towel is red and she looks like Little Red Riding Hood. Maybe she's bringing the truth to me in a basket!

"Truth or dare?" she asks.

"Dare," I say, feeling brave.

"Hmm." She thinks for a minute, tapping her finger on her mouth. "The closet in my dad's room. You have to go in there for five minutes with the light out."

"Five minutes?"

"Five minutes," she says. "It's not as bad as dipping your head in a freezing-cold lake!"

We get up and walk into her dad's room. There are pictures of Darby and her sister and brothers all over, but I notice that Darby's mom isn't in any of them. I want to ask Darby about her parents because Iris says she already knows. I decide to be brave.

"Are your parents getting divorced?" I ask her.

She spins around.

"No!" she says. "Who told you that?"

"Iris. She said—"

"I don't care what she said; it's not true! Iris is a liar and that's final."

She's squeezing her eyes shut again. Maybe she does that because she wants me to disappear.

"Okay," I say. "I'm glad it's not true. I don't think Iris is a liar, though. Maybe her mom just told her the wrong thing."

"Maybe," says Darby. "C'mon, get into the closet!"

She looks upset. I guess I would be, too, if someone asked me if my parents were getting divorced.

She opens the closet door. There are just a few clothes in there, a fishing net, a tackle box, and some big muddy boots. On the shelf is a cat skeleton.

"A cat skeleton? I'm not going in there with a cat skeleton!" I say.

"Oh, that's just our cat, Spooky," Darby says. "Dad loved that cat, so he saved her. Okay, get in there. A dare's a dare. I'll set the kitchen timer for five minutes."

She closes the door on me.

It's pitch-black. All I can think about is Spooky, the cat skeleton above my head. Who keeps a cat skeleton in the closet? A ghost-story writer, I guess. I start counting to help me feel less scared. *One Mississippi, two Mississippi* . . .

I hear a door open and close.

"Darby?" I say.

She doesn't answer.

. . . *Two hundred one Mississippi, two hundred two Mississippi* . . . It's the longest five minutes of my life. Finally, I hear the kitchen timer go off.

"Darby?" I say, afraid to move.

I don't hear anything. I open the closet and peek out.

"Darby?" I call.

Nothing. Now I'm scared. Where is she? She's going to jump out at me, I know it. I peek out of the bedroom and it's darker. The shades are closed.

"Darby?"

I want to cry now. I walk around the bedroom

door and go into the living room. I look past the typewriter into the kitchen and see Darby's foot on the floor by something red. Then I see the rest of Darby lying on her back, her glasses skewed and her face covered in . . . blood!

"Darby!" I shout, and run over to her.

"BOO!" she says, bolting up off the ground.

I scream.

"Gotcha," she says, smiling and licking blood off of her lips.

I notice a bottle of ketchup on the kitchen counter, which explains everything.

"Darby, that's so mean!" I say. "I thought you were—"

"BOO!" says a man who suddenly leaps out of the coat closet door at us.

"AHHHHH!" I scream again.

"Gotcha," Darby's dad says. He smiles at me, then gives me a bear hug. "I came home while you were in the closet, and Darby and I set up the scene. I hope we didn't scare you too bad."

I sit down by the popcorn and take a big breath.

"You got me," I say.

Darby's family is crazy! Luckily, it's time for Mom to pick me up. I hear a horn.

"Bye!" I say, grabbing my backpack and heading out the door. "Thanks!"

"See ya next time!" says Doug.

Maybe, I think. *Maybe not!* But I have to admit that it is pretty fun being scared like that.

I get in Vanna, and Mom and I splash down the bumpy driveway.

"Mom, are Darby's parents getting divorced?" I ask her.

"Yes, did she tell you?"

"No, she said they aren't. My friend Iris told me at school. Why didn't you tell me?"

"Darby's mom said Darby's having a hard time adjusting to the news, so she said it was better to keep it quiet for now. Sorry I didn't tell you."

"It's okay," I say. "But Darby says they aren't getting divorced."

"Maybe she's just taking a while to get used to the idea," Mom says.

"Why are they getting divorced?" I ask.

"I don't know," Mom says. "But Darby's mom says her dad's got a few skeletons in the closet."

"Really?" I say. "I only saw one."

Chapter 18
The Bad Black Hole Lie

It's finally Darby's turn to take home a rat for the weekend. And the best part? She's spending the night at my house!

Mom doesn't look too excited to have Riley back in our house, but we're careful all afternoon when we play with him, so he doesn't escape.

We do everything with Riley: He looks for frogs with us, he plays Monopoly, and he sits in Darby's lap eating popcorn while we watch a movie. Before bed, Darby even reads my old, beat-up copy of *Goodnight Moon* to him. She wants to sleep with him, too, but Mom comes in and says, "Nope. Nooo way!"

On Saturday morning, we wake up to the sound of Riley running on his wheel. He really is a health nut, just like Mom! I get Riley out of his cage. We make a big circle of stuffed animals on my bed and put Riley in the middle, then watch him run back and forth in the circle, sniffing, sniffing, sniffing.

"Do *not* let him get out!" says Darby. "I don't want to be the one who loses a rat!"

We watch Riley run in circles, twitching his nose and smelling everything.

"I think he smells breakfast," Darby says.

He does smell breakfast! We put Riley back into his cage and run upstairs. Mom made eggs and bacon.

"Is there something else to eat with my eggs, Mom, 'cause I told you, I'm not eating bacon!" I say.

"I got you some Fakin'," she says. "I heard it's not bad. We could try it."

Abby comes in with her pajamas and a cowboy hat, dragging her pink blankie behind her. Even though she's a know-it-all, she's still really cute.

"I want Fakin', too!" she says.

"What's the difference between vegan and vegetarian?" I ask Mom, looking at the word *vegan* on the Fakin' package.

"If you're vegetarian, you don't eat any meat. If you're vegan, you don't eat any animal products at all. No eggs, no butter."

"No butter?" we all say.

"Mmm, bacon!" Dad says, taking a piece of Fakin' from the plate.

He takes a bite.

"What is *this* stuff?" he asks.

"It's Fakin'," I say. "It's not that bad."

"Yeah, but it's not that good, either," says Dad, grabbing a piece of real bacon from Mom.

When we're done with breakfast, we head downstairs to play with Riley. It's a beautiful sunny day, the perfect kind for watching cartoons. We watch four in a row till Mom comes and ruins it and tells us to get outside.

We play under our deck for a while next to Mom, who is pulling weeds, her usual weekend activity. We make a little house out of sticks and leaves.

"It's Riley's house," I say.

"Perfect!" says Darby. "But it needs a sign with his name."

We write RILEY'S HOUSE on a piece of paper, tape it to a stick, and put the sign into the ground beside his house.

"We should go get him and put him inside," Darby says.

"I wish we could shrink so we could go in there with him," I say, imagining myself in a tiny little couch inside the house.

watching TV on a beautiful sunny day. (a.k.a. No Mom)

Then we go to my room to play with Riley some more. I take him out of his cage and hold him, and Darby and I take turns petting his head with one finger.

Darby leaves to go to the bathroom and closes the door to my room behind her. I put Riley on my lap and pet him. I'm sitting cross-legged, and suddenly he crawls down my leg onto my sock. Then, he turns around and starts to climb up my sock into my pant leg. I stand up to let Riley get out, but he climbs farther up my sock. I take a few steps and Riley hangs on, so I take a few more steps.

"Like the ride, Riley?" I say.

I start walking in circles. Suddenly Riley sticks a claw into my leg. It hurts and I jump, and when I do, he drops out of my pant leg onto the floor.

And I don't even want to say what happens next. I don't want to say it, but I will: I step on Riley.

"Riley? *Riley!* Oh no!"

He doesn't look right. I pick him up and he doesn't move at all, so I stick him back into his cage, and he just lies there. Maybe he'll wake up, I think. He can't be *dead*.

I open the door and yell down the hall. "Darby! Something's wrong with Riley!"

Darby runs out of the bathroom.

"What?"

She runs into the room and looks at Riley lying there.

"I think he's dead," I say.

Darby pokes him. He doesn't move. She tickles his feet. Nothing happens. Nothing at all. Why won't he just breathe or something? I didn't step on him that hard.

"What did you do?" Darby asks me, bursting into tears.

"I . . . I . . ." I don't know what to say. I don't want Darby to hate me. "I . . . I don't know."

"What do you mean you don't know?"

"I didn't do anything! He just died."

Uh-oh.

"He . . . he was eating his food, then I turned around. When I looked at him again, he was dead. I think his food might be poisonous or something."

Now I'm lying again! What's wrong with me? But I've already done it. I can't go back now.

Darby reaches into Riley's cage and picks him up. Then she puts him down and starts crying even harder. We run and tell Mom, who's still out pulling weeds.

"What happened?" she says, hugging us.

"Riley's dead!" we both say at the same time. I have the urge to say *jinx*, but I don't.

Darby is trying to stop crying. She's doing that hiccupping thing that happens when you cry for a long time. Her nose is running. Mom goes inside to get her a tissue.

"What happened to Riley?" asks Mom.

"We don't know," I say. "I just looked over and he was dead. I think he might have gotten poisoned by his food."

Uh-oh. Now I'm lying to Mom, too!

We go in the kitchen, and Mom makes us some tea. Darby can't stop crying. My stomach hurts. I feel awful about Riley, but I feel even worse that I lied to Darby and Mom. I can't tell them that I *killed* him, though. I play the whole thing over in my mind, only I change the story so that I put Riley back in the cage *before* he dies:

Riley suddenly stands up in his cage, grabs his heart with his paws, then drops dead. It makes me feel better to think about it like this. Wait! If I feel better, then this must just be a teeny-tiny lie. There's nothing wrong with a teeny-tiny lie!

Then I look at Darby. She's still crying. Her tears are dripping onto her nose, and her nose is dripping into her mouth. I realize that this *isn't* a teeny-tiny lie. Or a Big Bad Lie like hers. This is a **Big Bad Black Hole Lie**.

Mom suggests that we have a funeral and bury Riley in the yard.

"I want to take him home," Darby says.

I hope he doesn't end up in her dad's closet like Spooky. I don't even want to *think* about that.

We follow Mom down the hall, and she finds us a shoebox so Darby can take Riley home. We take it into my room. Riley is still lying at the bottom of his cage just like we left him. I was imagining—hoping—that we'd walk in and find that he was just playing dead.

"Can we put something in the box to make him more comfortable?" Darby asks me.

Even though he's not alive anymore, I want to make him more comfortable, too. Mom says we can use one of our hand towels, so we lay it on the bottom of the box. Darby picks up Riley. Her hands are shaking, and she's crying really hard.

I imagine pressing an undo button and going back to a few hours ago when Riley was still alive. I wouldn't stand up when he ran up my sock. I'd just sit there and let him crawl back out. Then none of this would have happened. I wouldn't step on him, I wouldn't lie about it, and Riley would still be a happy, healthy rat.

"How could he die?" Darby cries, a tear dripping onto Riley's fur.

I should tell her the truth. But I can't. I just can't.

"I don't know," I say.

Suddenly I realize I'm squeezing my eyes shut just like Darby does. I don't want to make Darby go away, though. I just want to make this whole thing go away. Maybe that's why she does it, too.

"But you were here!" Darby says.

"I know, but I was turned around. I didn't see it."

"Why weren't you watching him the whole time?" she asks me. "How could you turn around?"

"I—I d-don't know . . ." I stutter.

"Why aren't you crying?" she asks me. "Aren't you sad?"

"I'm really sad," I tell her.

I don't know why I'm not crying. I think I feel too sick to cry.

"Let's put some flowers around him," Darby suggests.

We go outside and pick little daisies and yellow dandelions from the grass and lay them on the towel around Riley. Then we get the sign we made for his house and put that beside him, too.

"We should say something before we put the lid on," Darby says.

I'm quiet, so Darby starts.

"R-Riley," she sobs. "You were . . . you were . . ."

She's crying so hard she can't talk.

"You . . . you do it," she says to me.

I have to say something. All I want now is to put the lid on and have Darby take Riley away. Looking at him lying there is making me too sad.

"We . . . we'll miss you, Riley," I say, choking up a little bit. "You were a good rat."

Then I start crying, too. I've never felt so sad before. I loved Riley, and I didn't mean for any of this to happen! A tear drops from my cheek onto Riley. Darby picks up the lid and puts it on the box. Then she calls her mom and goes home.

I go to bed early, but I can't sleep. I *killed* Riley. He's dead because of me. Worst of all, I lied about it. I said I would never lie, and now I have. Just like Deets. Just like Darby!

I make a promise to myself.

"I'll be braver at school on Monday," I whisper. "I will be *myself* again—I'll be the Lily who *doesn't* lie. On Monday, I'll tell Darby the truth."

Chapter 19

Rat Killer

I don't even eat any breakfast on Monday because I'm so nervous about going to school and telling the truth. Darby told me that her mom called Mrs. Larson yesterday to tell her what happened to Riley, and she's not mad, which makes me feel a little bit better. But I'm still terrified when the bus pulls into the parking lot.

Once we're all settled at our desks, Mrs. Larson breaks the news to the class.

"I have some sad news, class," she says.

Here we go. She clears her throat.

"Another one of our rats, Riley, is no longer with us. Unfortunately, he died over the weekend."

"He was my favorite rat!" Sonja starts crying.

"Who had him?" Mikey raises his hand after he asks the question.

"Mikey," says Mrs. Larson, "*who* had Riley is not important. What matters is that we are all able to talk about our feelings and—"

Billy leans over from his desk toward the rat cage and looks at the sign-up list.

"Darby had him!" he yells, pointing at Darby.

"You're not a Rat Whisperer," says Deets. "You're a Rat *Killer*!"

Half the class starts laughing—the half that's not crying.

"Deets, that is *not* necessary!" Mrs. Larson says. "Please be sensitive to Darby. It is *not* Darby's fault that Riley died. Please be kind. Sometimes things like this just happen."

Yeah, things like your best friend stepping on him, I think. *I should tell them now; I should tell them the tru—*

"What about our experiment?" Iris asks.

"I'm afraid that our experiment is over now," says Mrs. Larson. "I think we've collected enough data to show definitively that the health-food rats stayed healthier, and that's what we were trying to do. Now we will put our junk-food rats on a healthy diet, and they will be our class pets."

"But one of the health-food rats is missing, and now the other one is *dead*!" yells David. "All we really proved is that even if you only eat healthy food, you can still disappear or *die* before the person who eats whatever they want!"

"Yes," Mrs. Larson says. "Unfortunately, accidents happen; but to live life to its fullest, you'll do best to stay healthy."

"I'd rather eat junk food," says David.

Mrs. Larson looks exasperated.

Unfortunately, Mrs. Larson's speech about being kind to Darby doesn't stop anyone at recess.

"Rat Killer!" says Gabriella.

"Rat Killer!" yell Sonja and Tillie right after her.

Then someone else shouts, "Darby's a Rat Killer! Darby's a Rat Killer!" as they run by.

Some of the girls from our class are jumping rope, and they make up a song about her.

Darby, Darby, Cruella de Vil. How many pet rats can she kill? One, two, three, four, five...

The boys start chasing us, with Deets in the lead yelling, "Get the Rat Killer!"

They chase us across the four-square courts. I look down and see Darby's shoe is untied again. She needs Velcro shoes. No time to tie it now! They chase us to the springboards on the playground. Darby is ahead of me and runs over the top of the board and jumps off, but she steps on her own shoelace and falls flat on her face.

"Ow, ow, oweee!" she screams.

Everyone gathers around. Darby is crying and holding her arm. Mrs. 'Stache comes over and glares at all of us, then helps Darby up and takes her to the nurse.

Mrs. Larson gets a call from Darby's dad after lunch, right in the middle of our spelling test.

Darby broke her arm!

And it is my fault. It is my fault. It is my fault.

At last recess, I have to go for my last day in the RTC. Mrs. 'Stache is waiting for me and Deets. Today there is a third-grade boy in here, too. He's crying and sniffling.

"Stop it!" Mrs. 'Stache yells at the boy. "That sniveling is driving me bananas!"

Mrs. Rash really is a bully, even if she writes nice things in my journal.

Hi, Mrs. Rash,
It's Lily. I just told a lie. I can't write about it here because I have to keep it secret FOREVER, but I did it. I told a lie just like Darby did, I feel super, super-duper supercalifragilisticexpialadocius BAD about it. And now Darby broke her arm because of me. ME!
   This is how big my lie is.

Fantastic illustration, Lily!
-Mrs. R.

HELP ME!

How am I supposed to be mad at Darby for lying to me when now I lied to HER? I feel SO, SO BAD! I'm not a liar, but I lied! I CAN'T BELIEVE DARBY BROKE HER ARM AND IT'S MY FAULT! I'd better tell her the truth. I'll tell her tomorrow. I WILL!

★Please don't tell ANYONE about this, Mrs. Rash! ★
←Pretty please with sugar on top?
please

Lily, what you write in the RTC is confidential unless I have reason to worry about your or another's physical well-being. -mrs. R

P.S. 30 seconds left of my last day in the RTC forever and ever! It's been great hanging out with you. I'm not just saying that. You're nicer than you look!

Sincelery
Sincerely, Lily

I'm sure I'll see you here again, Lattuga. And... Thank you?
- Mrs. R

That last part was a teeny-tiny lie, but that's okay.

A few days later, Darby is back at school. She shows up for class five minutes late, right in the middle of the Pledge of Allegiance, with her arm in a yellow cast.

"Hi, everyone!" says Darby.

She goes to her seat to sit down. Everyone is asking her about her arm at the same time.

"Class!" says Mrs. Larson. "Darby may tell us what happened to her arm after the Pledge of Allegiance."

We finish the pledge, and Darby starts talking.

"The boys were chasing Lily and me at recess and calling me Rat Killer," she says. "We kept running, then we jumped up on the springboards to try to get away. I tripped, then flipped into the air, and did two full somersaults before I landed on my arm."

SPROING

"I didn't see any somersaults!" says Deets. "You're lying!"

She glares at Deets.

"I dislocated my elbow and fractured my wrist. Unfortunately, it was my left hand—so I can still do my homework."

Everyone laughs.

"I will have this cast on for six weeks. Does anyone want to sign it?"

Everyone jumps out of their seats.

"Class! Sit down!" Mrs. Larson says. "I will allow you to sign Darby's cast before we go out for first recess."

As soon as the bell rings, everyone gathers around Darby. Mrs. Larson makes us line up. Mikey is in the very front. Darby is smiling at him.

"Hi, Mikey," she says.

Mrs. Larson gives Mikey a marker. "As soon as each of you finishes signing Darby's cast, you may go outside."

Then she sits at her desk and puts on her glasses, which means she's going to grade papers or something.

Mikey steps up. He writes *RAT KILLER* so big it takes up half the cast, then he turns around and hands the pen to Sonja with a big grin on his face. Darby is still smiling, but as her best friend, I can tell she's not happy about what Mikey wrote.

Sonja draws a picture of a rat with X's for eyes and signs her name.

Deets draws a picture of a gravestone with *R.I.P. Riley* written on it, and Gabriella writes: *Get well soon, Dorkski.*

By the time everyone is done, most of Darby's cast is covered with dead rats and accusations. Darby looks like she might cry. When Mrs. Larson realizes what happened, she tries to clean off Darby's cast with wipes. All it does is smear the ink and make everything look even more dramatic.

I feel terrible because *I* should have RAT KILLER written all over me.

Everyone except Darby and me has to stay in for recess and clean their desks for writing unkind things on Darby's cast, which puts Darby into a better mood. We walk together to our invisible clubhouse. I bring my markers so I can try to make Darby's cast look better. We sit in our invisible chairs and say the Rizzlerunk pledge: *With loyalty and honesty for all.*

I'm going to tell her the truth, like I said I would.

"Darby, I . . ." I start.

But I can't do it! Now I've lied to everybody. My Big Bad Black Hole Lie has grown too big. So we sit in our invisible clubhouse with our big monster lies, and it feels extra crowded.

I do my best to make Darby's cast look nicer with some flowers and hearts, but it sort of makes the cast look even more tragic with the dead rats lying among a bunch of flowers.

After school we are going to Darby's house. I don't want to go. Darby buried Riley, and she wants to show me his grave.

On the bus, I try to act like everything is normal, but it's hard. I don't know how Darby has kept her lie with her for so long without telling me. Maybe she really thinks she didn't draw the picture of Michelangelo's *David*. I imagine my lie sitting on my lap, and it's so heavy that I can't talk. I just sit quietly and stare out the window.

We get to Darby's house, and she brings out Pop-Tarts, but I don't even feel like eating one.

"Are you sick or something?" she asks me.

"I have a stomachache," I say. "I'm a little afraid of seeing Riley's grave."

We go outside and pick a few flowers, then walk down the big grassy hill to a tree near the lake. Darby points down. It's Riley's grave.

"There it is," she says. She bends down, reaches her good arm out, and puts her flowers on top of it. "I miss you, Riley."

Darby told me about how her dad said she could keep Riley in his closet, so she could see him sometimes, but Katy wanted to have a funeral and bury him the way they do in movies. Darby said her whole family came and played music. I wish I could have seen it, but the truth is that I didn't want to go. Being with Darby's family with my Big Bad Black Hole Lie hanging on my back during the funeral would've been horrible.

♪ Riley never ate any bacon, but even vegetables couldn't save him... ♫

I bend down and put my flowers next to Darby's. "I'm sorry, Riley. I'm sorry you died. I miss you, too." My throat feels tight like I'm going to cry. I want to tell Darby the truth.

"Darby," I say. "I . . ."

But I still *can't do it*! Anyway, she lied first, I realize. She should admit it first. If I could just get *her* to tell the truth, then it would be easier for me to tell her about Riley, and this could *all be over*!

Chapter 20
Truth or Dare

On Monday, everyone is still calling Darby the Rat Killer. It doesn't help that it's still written all over her cast. I guess it wouldn't come off. It looks like her brother added to it, too.

Dumb Darby's not a cat, but she killed a rat!

—Kyle

Luckily, the bell rings, and it's time to sit down. Mrs. Larson makes everyone be quiet for the Pledge of Allegiance, but I hear Deets say, "And to the Rat Killers for which it stands . . ." Darby glares at him.

"This is fascinating, class," Mrs. Larson says, looking into the rats' cages. "Marshmallow and Ratsinburger have gone two days without eating a thing! I wonder what's wrong with them?"

We look inside our remaining rat cage. A bunch of cut-up sweet potatoes, some celery, and some sunflower seeds are still in the bowl, looking like Bacon's compost. After she told us we were stopping the experiment, Mrs. Larson threw the rest of Marshmallow and Ratsinburger's junk food into the trash. Later she found José and Mikey trying to sneak some of it out to eat during lunch break.

"Maybe they don't like the healthy food," Mikey guesses, "since all they've been eating is junky stuff."

"Oh, that couldn't be the case," Mrs. Larson tells us. "Their little bodies must be craving some decent nutrition. Maybe something was wrong with the food."

"Maybe it's like my brother!" José says. "Maybe they're so used to junk food, they won't eat anything else. My brother almost starved when my mom stopped letting him have junk food."

"It's a thought," Mrs. Larson says. "Or maybe the food has just gone bad."

She has us clean the cage and replace the food with new carrots and celery and seeds. But the next day the food is untouched, and the next day, and the next day, too.

"See, they're like my brother," José tells Mrs. Larson. "They'd rather starve than eat healthy food. I think we'd better give them the stuff they're used to before they die!"

We all agree, but Mrs. Larson wants the rats to eat the healthy food. So we wait.

At recess, Darby and I hide in the corner of the playground so no one will tease her.

"I think *you* should be getting called Rat Killer," Darby says.

"What? Why?" I ask. I get a sinking feeling in my stomach. Does she know?

"Because it was *your* house!" she says. "Maybe it was the smell of that Fakin' that killed him."

Again, I think about how good it would feel to let go of my Big Bad Black Hole Lie and tell her my secret. But what would happen? I want

to keep my best friend. Anyway, Darby lied to me, too, so why do I feel so bad about it? And she started it. Now we're even! But that dumb lie keeps hanging on my back.

Then I know what to do. Keep the truth or dare going! Even though I have a lie now, too, I'm not afraid to do truth, because Darby has no idea that I lied. Once she confesses about the drawing, I decide, I *will* tell her about Riley.

Darby comes over to my house on Saturday. We sit down on the edge of the lake and build frog houses.

"Want to play truth or dare?" I ask.

"Sure. I'll start this time," she says. "Truth or dare?"

"Truth," I say.

"Have you ever kissed a boy?" she asks me.

"That's an easy one! No," I say.

"Truth or dare?" I ask her.

"Dare," she says.

I try to think of something she won't do.

"I dare you to jump off the dock into the lake with your clothes on."

"No! You already made me dip my head in. It's freezing! Besides, I can't get my cast wet."

"Okay, then you have to do truth!"

"Fine, I'll wade in to my belly button," she groans.

Darby takes off her shoes, rolls up her pants, and steps off the bulkhead into the shallow water and walks a little deeper.

"It's freezing!" she says. "I'm going to get you back for making me do this!"

"Watch out for the drop-off!" I warn her.

But I say it a second too late. Darby takes a step over the drop-off, where the lake bottom suddenly falls away and gets much deeper. All I can see of her is her cast in the air, which she has somehow managed to keep dry.

She spins around and gets her foot back on the shallow ground, then lifts herself up so she's standing again. She looks like a swamp monster. Her glasses are crooked on her face, and she has a piece of algae on her head.

When she steps back up over the bulkhead and onto the grass, her teeth are chattering and her lips are kind of blue. She takes off her glasses and wipes them on her shirt, squinting without them.

"We need to get you into the shower to warm up," I say, taking her arm.

"I n-n-n-eed a bag over my c-c-ast," she says.

As she strips off her clothes in the bathroom, I run and get a plastic bag and a rubber band, then wrap her cast. After Darby takes her shower, I find her an outfit of mine since her clothes are all wet. My pants are too small for her, so she has to leave the button undone, and her ankles show.

Dad calls us for lunch.

"Waiting for a flood?" he asks Darby.

Mom's gone, so Dad gives us peanut butter sandwiches—regular ones *without* alfalfa sprouts. When we're done eating, I tell Darby it's my turn for truth or dare now.

"Truth or dare?" she asks me, smiling, probably ready to get me back for making her go in the lake.

"Truth," I say.

"You can't do truth every single time!" she says.

"Yes, I can," I tell her. "You do dare every single time. Anyway, after I stayed in your dad's skeleton closet, I don't ever have to do a dare again."

"Okay, fine. Have you ever stolen anything?" she asks me.

"I accidentally stole some cookies from the grocery store once when I was a little kid because they were in a box with a big clown face on it and I thought they were free," I say. "'But that's it. Since it was an accident, I don't count it as stealing. Truth or dare?"

"Dare," she says.

"Really?" I ask her. "After the lake? Why don't you ever do truth? There must be something you *really* don't want to tell me."

"No!" she says. "I just like dares better."

"Okay, fine. I dare you to cover your face in honey, then go outside and put grass on it."

"What? That's crazy. There are bees out there!"

"You want to do truth, then?" I ask her.

"Get the honey," she says.

We get a jar of honey out of the pantry, and I find a spatula.

"Do you have something to pull my hair off my face?" she asks.

My mom pays to have this done!

I go and get her a hair band. We pull her hair back, and she takes the spatula and smears honey all over her face, then she puts her glasses back on, so she can find the lawn.

"This is pretty fun!" she says, licking her face. "It tastes good, too."

We get honey all over the table and chair, Darby's hair, and the doorknob. Darby goes out to the lawn and puts handfuls of grass on her face.

"You're going to give me nightmares!" I say, which gives us an idea.

Darby hides in the pantry, and I call Abby upstairs.

"What?" Abby asks.

"Do you know where the sweet potato chips are?" I ask her.

"They're in the pantry," she says.

"Well, I couldn't find them. Can you look?"

Abby goes to the pantry door and grabs the knob.

"Why's it so sticky?" she asks.

"I don't know," I say.

She opens the door, and Darby jumps out at her.

Abby screams so loud that Dad comes up from the den.

"What in the world?" he says.

Abby is laughing, but Dad sounds kind of angry. Dad *is* kind of angry. I look at the kitchen, and I can see why. There's grass stuck to the table, chair, floor, and doorknob. Snort is licking the floor, and her fur is getting stuck on the leg of the chair. We spend the next hour cleaning up after ourselves. By then, Darby's clothes are dry, so Dad makes her go home.

Still no success getting Darby to do truth. Maybe the only way I'll ever get her to admit to her Big Bad Black Lie is to admit mine first.

Chapter 21

Pig Rescue

A week later, Darby's cast still has mean things written all over it, and the nickname Rat Killer has stuck. And I *still* haven't told her the truth. My Big Bad Black Hole Lie is hanging on to me and getting heavier and heavier.

At least there's some good news at school.

"The rats have eaten!" Mrs. Larson exclaims. "Honestly, I was worried they might just die of starvation, but finally, after a week of protesting a decent meal, they've given in."

"You're amazing, Mrs. Larson!" says José. "When my brother wouldn't eat healthy food, my mom gave in after two days. She told Grandma she couldn't stand to watch him starve. But you watched them starve and didn't do *anything* about it!"

"Well, José," Mrs. Larson says, her smile fading a bit. "I would not have let them starve to *death*, but I am happy to say that I didn't have to make that decision. They've eaten their food, and I think they're back on track to be in good health!"

"But you said you thought they would die of starvation!" says Billy.

"I did, Billy, but I wouldn't have let it happen," she says. "Back to your seats, everyone! Long division test!"

Over the next few days, our class is amazed at the changes to Ratsinburger and Marshmallow. They're climbing around the cage, hopping (which Mrs. Larson tells us is called *popcorning*),

Popcorning

and running almost nonstop on their wheel. Their noses and eyes are shinier, and their fur looks smoother. They look like the rats that we got at the beginning of the experiment, only better! They're super rats!

At recess, as Darby and I walk to the invisible clubhouse, I feel like we must look so heavy with our lies riding on our backs, but nobody but me seems to notice. Maybe Darby locked hers in a box in her garage and doesn't even carry it around with her. I should try that.

We say our Rizzlerunk pledge, which doesn't feel very good at this point.

"Let's do *the thing* after school," Darby says.

"What *thing*?" I ask.

"Rescue Bacon! I think today is the day."

I sniff the air.

"You're right," I say. "I smell victory!"

After school, Darby comes over.

"Mom, we're going to feed the pigs today!" I tell her as we walk in the door.

"Feed the pigs? Really?" Mom says. "That would be *great*! It's been a long time since you fed them last."

It's true—Darby and I haven't gone to see Bacon for a long, long time. Mom feeds him herself now, since we've all reminded her over and over that it was her idea to get a pig.

We get the compost from under the sink. It smells *sooo* bad. Darby and I do rock, paper, scissors to see who has to carry it.

"Paper beats rock! I win," I say.

"Two out of three," says Darby.

She wins. I carry the compost to the rowboat, then fetch a couple of pillowcases from my room. We get the oars, put on our life jackets, and untie the boat. It takes us more than an hour to row across the lake because the wind is blowing against us and I'm the only one who can row, since Darby has a cast on.

We finally get to the end of the lake and tie up the boat. We do two-out-of-three rock, paper, scissors again, and this time I win, so Darby has to carry the compost from the boat all the way to the pigs.

"I'm so tired," she says.

She sets the bucket down.

"Nice try, Darby," I say. "You lost two out of three."

"I know, but I have a broken arm."

I give in and carry it.

We get to Mrs. Swanson's house and knock on the door to be polite, but no one answers, so we walk around the side of the house to see the pigs. We stop at the gate.

"Where are they?" I ask.

"Maybe the Swansons *ate* them," says Darby.

"Stop it, Darby! They wouldn't do that without telling us!"

We open the fence and dump the yucky compost into the muddy trough.

"I am *so* glad I'm not a pig," Darby says, looking at the rotting vegetables.

"Me, too," I say. "I'd rather eat plain quinoa than that disgusting stuff."

"Bacon!" I call. "Baaaacon!"

Nothing.

"SOOO-EEEEY!" Darby yells.

Still nothing. We open the gate and walk across the muddy dirt and into the trees. I think Mom said the fenced-in area is two acres, and it's mostly forest and bushes. The pigs could be anywhere.

"SOOO-EEEEY!" we call some more.

Then we hear crunching. We look up. The three pigs are running toward us. Only, they

aren't tiny little piglets anymore. They are *huge*—
I could swear they're the size of Darby and me
put together! I realize where we are standing . . .
between them and the trough.

"RUN!" I shout.

We both turn and run as fast as we can. The
pigs sound like a whole herd of wild horses
behind us. Darby trips and gets back up so fast,
I hardly know what happened. We get to the
fence, throw open the gate, and run through it.
The pigs don't even stop for food. Darby trips
and falls again, splashing into a puddle.

"Darby, look out!" I yell.

She rolls out of the way of the monstrous pigs just in time, then gets up onto her hands and knees. We watch the snorting, squealing pigs run away from us.

I look down at Darby on the ground. She looks like a mud monster.

"Get up!" I yell. "We have to get them!"

Chapter 22

Fireman Frank

Darby and I run as fast as we can to try to herd the pigs back into their sty, but every time we get near them, they run in the other direction. We zigzag back and forth, until the pigs suddenly turn and take off down the road into the neighborhood. We sprint in the same direction as the pigs, but we lose sight of them. It feels like we've been running forever.

"What's that?" Darby says, stopping.

"A siren," I say. "Oh, no!"

A fire truck turns down the street.

"It can't be for us!" Darby says.

But it is! The fire truck stops, and Mikey Frank's dad, Fireman Frank, gets out.

"We got a call about some pigs on the loose," he says. "Have you two seen any pigs?"

Darby is shaking her head no. I want to shake my head no, but instead I nod yes. I already have one Big Bad Black Hole Lie hanging on my back— I don't want another one. Darby looks at me, then nods yes, too. Her eyes get watery, and her lip starts quivering.

"We were trying to rescue Lily's pig, Bacon, because we didn't want him to be bacon," she cries.

"We thought we could fit him inside this pillowcase," I say. "But the pigs got huge! They almost ran us over, then took off out of the gate."

"Hey, aren't you two in Mikey's class?" Fireman Frank asks.

Oh, no! He recognizes us.

"Don't worry, we'll find them," he says. "Are they your pigs?"

"One of them," I say. "The two others belong to Mrs. Swanson, my sister's teacher."

Fireman Frank asks Darby and me for our parents' phone numbers, then goes to his truck to contact them.

"We are so busted," I say.

Darby's mom shows up first. She gets out of her car.

"Darby and Lily, what in the world is going on?" she asks us.

We tell our story.

"Oh, boy. Hams on the lam," she says, and starts giggling.

I don't get it. But Fireman Frank obviously does, because he starts giggling, too. I think Darby's mom is flirting with Fireman Frank. Darby glares at her, but I don't know why because

Darby acts exactly the same way around Mikey.

Darby's dad rides up on his bike, and we have to tell the whole story over again. He looks annoyed that Darby's mom is laughing with Fireman Frank.

Then Mom pulls up in Vanna.

"Lily Lattuga, what on *earth* have you done?" she asks.

Her face is the color of the fire truck.

"I'm sorry!" I start crying. "I didn't want Bacon to become bacon. We tried to catch him in a pillowcase so we could let him go into Darby's woods, but we didn't know how huge the pigs had gotten. They almost trampled us!"

"SOOO-EEEEY!" Mom starts yelling. "SOOO-EEEEY!"

"Mom, stop!" I say. I bury my face in my hands.

SOOO-EEEEY!

OMG

Fireman Frank picks up his radio.

"They've been spotted!" he says. "Let's go."

He gets into his fire truck, turns on the siren, and heads down the street. We all get into Vanna and follow him.

I can't believe it! The fire truck stops in front of Deets's house! Deets is standing in the driveway with his dad and another kid, who must be his older brother. We all scramble out of the car after Fireman Frank.

Then a truck pulls up. A woman jumps out. A short, round woman with Brillo Pad hair, wearing a tan uniform, carrying a loop on a stick. It's Mrs. 'Stache!

"Animal control!" she yells.

Then a van screeches up.

"It's Marty Manchester from the news," Darby says, pointing at the van and jumping up and down.

Marty gets out of the van with a team of people carrying cameras and microphones.

"Rolling!" says the camerawoman.

"This is Marty Manchester reporting live from the scene of the swine." He flashes his white teeth at his own joke. "A trio of large hogs have escaped and are running rampant through the Hidden Marsh neighborhood."

Deets's dad starts yelling.

"They're in my garden! In the back! Those pigs are eating my prizewinning rhododendron bushes. I have the best rhododendrons in the country, and they're ruining them! I'll sue whoever did this!"

"Lead me to the pigs," says Fireman Frank.

"This way," Deets says, turning to run through the gate to his backyard.

Mr. Frizzle pushes past Deets. "Me first, Deets!"

Then Deets's brother pushes Deets down onto the grass and follows his dad.

"Dumb Deets," he snarls.

Deets looks like he might cry. Darby and I look at each other. Deets makes it really hard to be nice to him, but I think both Darby and I decide at the same time that it's what we have to do. Darby holds out her good hand and helps him up.

We follow Fireman Frank and Mrs. 'Stache into the yard, with the news team following. We enter the yard just in time to see the last pig butt squeezing under the fence where the pigs have dug a hole. There are leaves and branches all over the lawn. Deets's little shih tzu is jumping up and down by the fence, yapping nonstop.

Deets's dad is jumping up and down, too, with a long stream of inappropriate words spewing from his mouth.

Everyone stares for a moment, then Fireman Frank turns and runs back to his truck.

Mrs. 'Stache follows him.

"Animal control! Out of my way!" she yells.

"It's the perfect job for Mrs. 'Stache!" Darby says.

Mom turns and runs after her, yelling, "SOOO-EEEEY!"

We all turn and follow Mom. We can see the three pigs running down the street toward the lake road, dust clouding up behind them. I never knew pigs were so fast! We jump back into Vanna and follow Fireman Frank, Mrs. 'Stache, and the pigs. They're headed toward Darby's house! As we approach her driveway, we see a police car drive up from the other direction and slam on the brakes. Two police officers jump out and leap at the pigs, but the pigs swerve around them, veering into Darby's gate and down her driveway toward the lake.

We hop out of Vanna, and the whole lot of us chases them on foot down the driveway, except Mrs. 'Stache, who keeps on driving. She slams on her brakes by the house, barely missing the squealing pigs, who speed like runaway trains down the grassy hill.

Mrs. 'Stache throws open her door and follows them on foot, right on their tails, as the pigs run straight onto Darby's dock and leap impressively off the end. A huge splash of water drenches Mrs. 'Stache and the dock. Mrs. 'Stache tries to stop, but the wet dock is slippery—and she slides right off the end!

"Oh, no," Darby and I say together.

"Are you getting this?" Marty Manchester asks the camerawoman.

She gives him a thumbs-up.

We all run to the dock and watch the pigs swim away toward the swamp, followed by Mrs. 'Stache, who is a much better swimmer than she is a runner, even fully dressed with boots on. That lady is full of surprises.

"SOOO-EEEEY!" yells Mom.

"Too late, Mom!" I say.

"I think that they're headed toward the blueberry farm," says Darby's mom. "Maybe they're going back to their sty for food."

We all pile back into Vanna and drive to Mrs. Swanson's house to wait. When we pull up, Dad and Abby are in the driveway with Mr. and Mrs. Swanson.

"Oh, Lily," Dad says.

"SOOO-EEEEY!" yells Mom.

"Mom," I say. "Stop! It's not working!"

"Yes, it is," she says.

We see the three pigs turning the corner on the street, chased by a very wet Mrs. 'Stache. The pigs run past us, around the house, and back into the sty. Mr. Swanson closes the gate behind them.

"They'll always come back for food," he says.

Mrs. Swanson runs into her house and comes out with a towel for Mrs. 'Stache, who seems like she might pass out from breathing so hard.

"Well, looks like my work's done," says Fireman Frank. "Let's keep these hams where they belong, shall we, girls?"

"Yes, Fireman Frank," we both say.

"See you later, Mary," he says, winking at Darby's mom.

"I hate Mikey Frank," says Darby. "And his dad."

"Well, looks like this hog-wild chase has an ending happier than a pig in slop," says Marty. "This is Marty Manchester signing off until next swine. Ha ha!"

I ride home with Dad and Abby. Dad lectures me for less than a minute before he starts laughing. The three of us laugh all the way home.

After dinner, Mom, Dad, Abby, and I all gather around the TV to watch the news. We see Deets get knocked aside by his dad, then pushed over by his brother.

"I feel really sorry for Deets," I say.

"But he's such a bully!" Abby says.

"No one deserves to be treated like that by a parent," Dad says. "It's no wonder he's mean. Try showing him a little kindness at school. It might work wonders."

Next we see Vanna racing down Pine Lake Road, Mrs. 'Stache in front of us, and the fire truck in the lead. Then we see Mrs. 'Stache run down the hill and slide off the dock after the pigs.

Abby rolls on the floor laughing, tears streaming from her eyes.

"Good news, Marty," says Susan the co-anchor. "We posted this segment online earlier this evening, and we've received several offers from organizations who want to buy these pigs to save them from the slaughter."

"It's true," says Mom. "Mrs. Swanson already received an offer from someone who has a hog sanctuary called Hog Heaven. They want to buy Bacon and the other pigs and are willing to pay quite a price."

"Will you sell him?" I ask Mom.

"I think so," she says. "Maybe I'll take the money and invest it in Fakin'!"

"Well, you and Darby certainly saved our Bacon, Lily," says Dad.

Abby hugs me.

"Thanks, Weewee," she says.

Don't call me Weewee!

Chapter 23
The Last Rat

The next day at school, we see the news segment on SHTV, including the part where Deets gets pushed around by his family. When the video shows Mrs. 'Stache slide into Pine Lake, Mrs. Larson starts laughing so hard she spits her coffee on her desk.

"It's going to be a fun day in the teachers' lounge!" she says, laughing.

"I did it," Deets says. "I saved the pigs!"

"You did not, Deets," says Gabriella. "We all saw what happened."

Iris looks at Deets, who's turning red.

"Way to go Lily, Darby, and Deets!" she says.

Everyone claps for us, and Deets almost smiles.

As soon as we walk out for recess, kids start teasing Deets for getting pushed down by his brother. Deets is getting riled up and looks like he might hit someone. Iris veers from her path to the library and stands next to him.

Leave Deets alone, you **BULLIES!** Can't anyone be nice around here? Recess would be a lot more **FUN!**

"Deets is the bully!" shouts Gabriella. "And a liar!"

"Maybe he just needs a real friend," Iris says.

She tries to put her arm around Deets's shoulders, but he shrugs her off and runs away. The group turns to follow him.

"You're awesome, Iris," Darby says. "Will you come to the invisible clubhouse with us today?"

"I'm almost done with my book," says Iris. "I think I'll go to the library to finish it."

"Come on, Iris! Please?" I ask her. "We want you to be in our club."

"Well," she says, "I guess I could try it out."

So she does. We teach her the Rizzlerunk pledge. Then, when we're just in the middle of teaching her the secret handshake, Abby wanders by with some friends.

"Heeere, kitty, kitty!" they are all calling. "Heeere, kitty!"

One of the little girls is crying.

"What's happening, Abby?" I ask her. "Why are you calling for a kitty?"

"Her new kitten got lost," she tells me, pointing to the crying girl. "She brought him for show-and-tell, and he got away. He escaped outside."

The little girl starts bawling even harder.

"What does he look like?" I ask.

"He's tiny and black and fluffy and has gween eyes and a black nose, and he's weally, weally cute," the girl tells us.

"Okay, we'll look for him," we tell them.

We spend the rest of recess searching the playground for the kitten, but we can't find him. Then the bell rings, and we run to class. As we enter the room, we see a fuzzy little black ball on top of the rats' cage.

"The kitten!" Darby says.

The cage is open and Ratsinburger is still there, but Marshmallow is gone.

"He ate Marshmallow!" David yells.

Sonja starts to cry. Mrs. Larson comes in with a cup of coffee that she's trying not to spill.

"Seats, everyone!" she says. "You know if I'm not here when you get back to the classroom, you need to—"

Suddenly, Mikey yells:

The cat ate the RAT!

Mrs. Larson sets down her coffee and moves toward the cage.

"It's a first-grader's kitten," I tell Mrs. Larson. "She lost him during show-and-tell, and she was looking for him at recess with my sister."

"It's a *monster* kitten!" Sonja cries.

Mrs. Larson picks up the kitten, who gazes up at her with his adorable green eyes. I can hear him start purring all the way from my desk.

"Oh, boys and girls," Mrs. Larson says, "*that* is impossible. This tiny little kitten is the same size as Marshmallow. There's no way it could have eaten the rat. Marshmallow must have escaped."

"It's Marshmallow's tail!" shouts Mikey, pointing to the ground.

"Cool!" says José.

Gabriella screams.

Mrs. Larson looks down, and, sure enough, there is the end of a rat tail on the ground.

"Oh, dear," says Mrs. Larson. "Children, I know you're upset. Please sit down."

We sit down. A few kids are crying harder now.

Mrs. Larson gets a paper towel and picks up the rat tail in one hand, still holding the kitten in the other.

"I will be right back," she says.

We all get up when she leaves and look around the classroom to see if we can find the rest of Marshmallow, but no one can find him.

When Mrs. Larson returns, we sit down and she talks to us.

"I am so sorry about Marshmallow," she says. "It is a terrible thing that happened, and I feel awful you had to be a part of it."

"All that's left is Ratsinburger," David says.

"Yes," Mrs. Larson says. "It looks like Ratsinburger is the sole survivor of our experiment.

I suppose I'll find a different nutrition project next year. This one certainly didn't turn out as planned."

"I think that would be wise," says Darby.

Chapter 24

More Truth or Dare

"Truth or dare?" Darby asks me on the bus on the way home after school.

"Truth!" I say.

"Why do you keep doing truth? You're really no fun to play with!" Darby says. "Hmmm . . . I have to think of a good one . . . I know . . . Have you ever lied to me?"

I feel myself get hot. My face must look like a huckleberry. I can't lie again.

"Yes," I say, feeling my stomach do a flip.

"You have?" she says. "About what?"

"That's a new question! Only one question," I tell her.

The bus stops, and we get off with Abby.

"Truth or dare," I say as we walk across the street.

"Tru . . . No. Dare," Darby says.

"You almost said truth!" I say. "Why'd you change your mind?"

"I've told you a million times! I just like dares better!" Darby says.

"Okay," I say. "I dare you to stand in the yard in front of Zach for three minutes."

"Are you serious?" she asks.

"Yep!" I say. "Abby and I will keep watch, and when we're done counting to a hundred and eighty, you can leave the yard."

RAGH RAGH RAGH

"That's mean!" Abby says. "Zach is the scariest dog in the whole world!"

"He is scary," Darby says. "But he's behind a pretty tall fence. I'm not worried. I'll do it."

217

We get off the bus and walk the trail toward Zach's yard. Zach hears us before we even round the corner and starts barking like a crazed killer dog. When he sees us, he bares his teeth. Slobber starts dripping from the sides of his mouth like we're a bunch of walking hot dogs.

"I hope he doesn't have rabies or something!" Darby says.

"Me, too. For your sake," I say.

"Good luck, Darby!" says Abby. She looks scared.

Darby runs to the middle of the lawn and stands there.

"One Mississippi, two Mississippi, three Mississippi . . ." Abby and I count out at the top of our lungs.

Zach starts taking running leaps at the fence as soon as Darby steps onto the lawn. He's getting higher and higher with each leap. He looks like he'll shred Darby like a newspaper if he gets hold of her.

"Count faster!" Darby yells.

"Thirty Mississippi, thirty-one Mississippi," Abby and I count.

Zach is leaping so high now, he's almost coming up to the top of the fence.

"Lily, he might make it over," Abby says.

"Don't worry," I tell her. "If he could make it over, he already would have."

"I have to pee!" Darby says. "Count faster!"

"Eighty-eight Mississippi, eighty-nine . . ."

All of a sudden, Zach's flying leap clears the top of the fence. He did it! He tumbles onto the ground. Darby drops her backpack like she's going to run, but then she just stands there frozen like Michelangelo's *David*.

"Darby, run!" Abby and I shout. "Run!"

Abby starts crying. Zach gets on his feet and looks straight at Darby. Then he surprises all of us.

He yelps, turns around, puts his paws up on the fence, and starts whimpering. He looks back at Darby and then starts running back and forth along the fence as if he wants to get back in.

Darby finally moves. She picks up her backpack and sprints toward us. We all run full speed ahead into my house and flop onto the living-room floor.

"Did you see that?" Darby says. "He's just a big baby! He's got about as much guts as a little bunny rabbit! He acts like a killer hyena all the time, but really he's just a big chicken-dog!"

We are all rolling on the floor laughing now.

"You're amazing, Darby," I tell her. "I would have been way too scared to do that. I wouldn't have cared *what* I don't want to tell the truth about."

Chapter 25

Super Rats

The next day, we come to school and see Mrs. Larson's rear end sticking out from the cabinet under the sink.

"What are you doing in there?" shouts David, running over to her.

She jumps and bumps her head on the pipes.

"David," she says, pulling herself out from under the cabinet and rubbing her head, "please keep your voice down!"

"What were you doing in there?" he asks her again.

"Seats!" she yells.

After we're all seated, we have to stand again for the Pledge of Allegiance.

"Indivisible," we all say, "with liberty and justice for—"

"RATSINBURGER'S GONE!" Mikey yells.

Everyone runs to the rat cage.

"How'd he get out?" Sonja asks, starting to cry. "Was it that kitten again?"

"I'll tell you when you get back to your seats, boys and girls," says Mrs. Larson.

When we're all settled, Mrs. Larson tells us the story.

"I came in this morning, and his cage was wide open," she says. "Don't worry, it wasn't a kitten—or any other kind of animal. Our classroom door was locked when I left last night, and the room was empty. Ratsinburger's cage was closed. I check it every night before I leave, so I know it wasn't us who left it open. I asked Ms. Wetherall, our janitor, if she might have opened it to clean the cage, and she looked at me like I was a little bit crazy. She said with a whole school to clean, she wouldn't bother with a rat cage."

"Good point," says Darby.

"The only thing I can come up with," Mrs. Larson continued, "is that darned rat got smart enough to open the cage by himself!"

"That's because he's a Super Rat!" Billy shouts.

"Billy, I have the floor," Mrs. Larson reminds him. "May I continue?"

Billy nods.

"So, I looked everywhere, and then I saw him run under our sink," she continues. "I put my head in there to find him, but he must have found a crack in the wall, because he was gone. Class, I don't know *where* that rat is. Please keep your eyes open. Now, as you know, we have a spelling test first thing this morning, so please take out your pencils and paper."

Mrs. Larson looks around the room as she says this. I can tell she's kind of jumpy like Mom was with Riley.

"Benign," Mrs. Larson says.

We all scribble the word *benign* in various spellings. That's a hard one. In my opinion, it should be an eighth-grade word, not a fourth-grade word.

"Necessary," says Mrs. Larson.

We all giggle.

"Class," she says "that is not . . . oh, I see."

She smiles.

We all start to attempt to spell *necessary* when Darby yells.

"It's Ratsinburger! It's Ratsinburger!"

Mrs. Larson's heels tip sideways, and she stumbles toward the closet and grabs a broom.

"Don't kill him!" yells Sonja.

He runs right across the room under all of our desks and into the coatroom. Mrs. Larson goes in there for a while and comes out with her hair out

of place and her cheeks all red.

"He's disappeared again, class," she tells us.
"Now, back to your seats. We must finish our
test."

At lunch, there's a scream.

"Rat, rat, rat!" shouts Deets.

Ratsinburger comes running
down the table with a Life Saver in
his mouth, weaving in and out of
our lunches.

"I got him!" Darby says.

She takes her lunch bag and slams it down
around Ratsinburger, turns it over, folds the top,
and presses it shut.

"I did it!" says Darby, holding the bag tight to
her chest.

Everyone starts clapping, until someone at the
kindergarten table screams. We look over. It's
another rat—and part of its tail is missing! The
rat is running down the kindergarten table with
an Oreo cookie in its mouth.

"It's Marshmallow!" shouts Tillie.

"No way," says Darby.

Marshmallow is making a run for it. Principal Walker, who is the size of a pro wrestler, is at the door. He lets out a little scream and jumps out of

the way as Marshmallow sprints onto the playground.

"Well, Marshmallow's gone for good," Darby says.

Darby, Iris, and I bring Ratsinburger back to the classroom and put him safely in his cage, then go out to recess.

"Are you coming to the Rizzlerunk Club again, Iris?" Darby asks.

"Maybe," she says, "if it's okay with you."

"Are you going to drop out of the Nobody Club?" I ask her.

"I don't know," she says. "Can I read my book in the invisible clubhouse?"

"You can do whatever you want," Darby says.

"Okay," Iris says. "I'll come."

We are sitting in the dirt, saying our pledge, when I see Marshmallow scurry by our clubhouse. She's got a piece of bacon in her mouth.

"That proves it!" Darby says. "Bacon is better than Fakin'. He could've stolen Iris's lunch, but he didn't!"

At the end of the day, when everyone is leaving the class, Darby goes up to Mrs. Larson's desk. For a second, I think she's going to tell Mrs. Larson that she's the one who drew the picture of *David*. But then she points to Ratsinburger in his cage. I walk over and stand by her.

"Can I have Ratsinburger as a pet?" she asks Mrs. Larson. "'Cause I'm the one who caught him today, and if I didn't, he'd be gone anyway. I'll take good care of him."

"Well, to be honest, I would be very happy to get Ratsinburger out of our classroom at this point," Mrs. Larson says. "But to be fair, I think we'd need to discuss this with the class. Maybe draw names from a hat."

"But the rest of the class called me Rat Killer!" Darby says. "They wrote it on my cast, and I didn't do anything. I didn't kill the rat! It just died!"

Darby looks like she might cry. I feel terrible again. I can't believe I still haven't told her the truth.

"You have a point, Darby," Mrs. Larson tells her. "I think I could make a case for you to the rest of the class."

"Ratsinburger is mine!" she tells me.

Darby's coming over after school so Mom picks us up with the rat and all the supplies.

"Want to play with Ratsinburger?" Darby asks me when we get to my house.

"No!" I say. "I'd rather do something else." *Anything else,* I say to myself. "I think he's had a long day. We should let him take a nap."

"Good idea," Darby says. "Let's look for frogs instead."

We get a bucket and head to the lake.

I promise to love him and pet him and hug him and **SQUEEZE** him.

Chapter 26

The Truth

The truth

"Truth or dare?" I say to Darby.

We're out at recess, and it's sunny and warm, so we are lying on the ground in our invisible clubhouse—just Darby and me. Iris has been coming to the clubhouse sometimes, but other times, like today, she decides to go to the library. She said it's kind of hard to read with Darby and me talking all the time. We get it. She can be in the Rizzlerunk Club *and* the Nobody Club if she wants to.

"Dare," Darby says.

"What a surprise!" I say sarcastically.

But I'm excited. I've been thinking about this one for a while.

"Okay. I dare you to chase Mikey around the playground, and when you catch him, you have to tell him you love him in front of everyone. I'll help you catch him."

"No!" says Darby. "*No, no, no!* I don't like Mikey anymore! His dad was acting weird with my mom. Plus, I saw his dad's name on her phone. Like, I think he called her."

"You mean they're dating?" I ask.

"No!" Darby says. "She wouldn't do that!"

"Okay," I say, "then how about you have to tell Deets you love him?"

"No," Darby says.

"I don't blame you," I say. "I thought he might start acting nicer after the pig thing, when Iris was nice to him, but I think he's only gotten meaner."

"It's like my mom said," says Darby. "No matter how much a snake sheds its skin, it's still a snake."

"Oh, I get it. That's a good one," I say. "But I don't know. I think we should keep being nice to him and see what happens."

"We can try," Darby says.

"So, are you going to take the dare?" I ask her. "Maybe some kindness is all he needs, like my dad said!"

"No," she says.

"Okay, then. Truth!"

"I don't want to play anymore. I don't like this game," she tells me.

"Then I win the game!"

She looks at me like a trapped rat.

"Fine!" she says. "I'll do truth."

"You will?" I say.

I'm shocked. I thought I'd never get her to do truth! But I'm ready.

"Truth," I say. "Did you draw the picture of Michelangelo's *David* that Billy gave to Mrs. Larson and then tell Mrs. Larson that I drew it?"

"No! I already told you that!" Darby says, even redder than she was at the thought of telling Mikey that she loved him.

"Come on, Darby," I say. "You know that *I know* you drew that picture."

"I did not!" Darby says again, squeezing her eyes shut as she says it. "It wasn't mine. We've already talked about this a gazillion times. I thought it was yours!"

"Darby!" I say. "You can't make something disappear just because you squeeze your eyes shut! You lied and you know it. I get it. I know what it's like to want something to be different."

She opens her eyes and looks startled, like she didn't know she'd shut them in the first place.

"Okay, how about this?" I say, getting ready to be the bravest I've ever been in my whole life, getting ready to get rid of my Big Bad Black Hole Lie. "If I tell you what *I* lied to *you* about—then will you tell me the truth about the picture?"

"It's a trick," Darby says. "You never lie."

"It was a big one," I say. "The biggest lie I've ever told. A *Big Bad Black Hole Lie.* And I'll tell you what it is—but only if you tell me that you drew the picture."

"Okay. Pinkie swear," she says.

How to do a pinkie swear. by Lily
1. Lock pinkies.
2. Swear.*

*Just kidding!

"So . . ." I say. "Truth! You drew it. Say it. I'm not going to be mad."

"It's just . . ." Darby says, closing her eyes. "You know how you said that just because you say something is true doesn't make it true? Well, I'm tired of pretending—"

"Pretending that my *David* was as bad as yours?"

"Ha ha," she says. "No. Pretending about my dumb parents. They're . . . they're getting divorced. I've been trying to pretend like they aren't, but they are."

"I'm sorry."

"And just because you *think* something is true, even if you think it's true as hard as you can, it *still* doesn't make it true."

"I'm sorry," I say again. "I know what you mean about wanting to change the truth."

"Why, are your parents getting divorced, too?" she asks me.

"No," I say.

"Oh, good," she says. "Because I like your house the way it is. Anyway, I'm sorry for lying. I wanted it to go away . . ."

"The divorce?"

"Yeah," she says, surprised.

I'm glad that Darby's telling me the truth about her parents, but now she looks upset. How am I supposed to get her to tell me the truth about the drawing, too? I decide to try.

"And the drawing?" I ask.

"Oh, that . . ." she stops. "I . . . I . . ."

Her lip starts quivering like she's going to cry.

"It's okay," I say. "I'm not going to be mad."

Her eyes are all wet. She looks down at her shoes again.

"We don't *have* to play anymore," I tell her. "It's fine."

"No, I'll say it," she says. "I drew the picture."

"You did?" I can't believe she said it.

"You know I did!" she says. "I didn't want to get in trouble, so I said you did it without thinking, and then I couldn't take it back. I wanted it to be the truth, so I pretended like it was true. But it didn't work. I drew it. I lied. I got you in so much trouble. I'm sorry!"

"I can't believe you finally told me the truth!"
I say.

I put my arm around her shoulder.

"I'm not mad," I tell her. "And I'm sorry about
your parents. That sucks."

She wipes her tears and nose on her sleeve. A
booger stretches from her nose and then breaks.

"That's disgusting," I say, smiling.

"Well?" she says. "Your turn! What did you lie
to me about?"

My smile turns over. Now I have to tell her the
truth, too! I don't know if I can do it.

"Tell me your lie," she says. "And this better
not have been a trick!"

"Okay," I say. "I will."

I take a big breath. I realize that this is it. I'm
going to unstick the truth. *I'm going to tell her!*

I lean in to her ear and whisper. . . .

I
killed
the
rat.

"WHAT?" Darby screams.

"Darby! Shhh. I killed Riley! I stepped on him by accident when he clawed me, and I didn't know what to do, so I stuck him back in his cage. It was an accident, but I killed him. It was me. I'm the real Rat Killer! I just felt so awful. I couldn't believe it. I mean, I killed an animal. . . . I killed our *friend*."

Saying it out loud is horrible.

"Poor Riley," she says. "You stepped on him?"

"I know," I say, shuddering.

"But, wait. How could you not tell me? I can't believe you didn't tell me!" she says way too loudly. "How could you lie about it like that?"

"I don't know," I say. "I'm sorry. I just didn't know what to do. I was really—I just felt horrible, and once I lied, I didn't know how to change my story. Then you broke your arm, and everyone started calling you Rat Killer, and everything just went crazy. Are you mad?"

"Of course I'm mad! I'll probably be called Rat Killer for the rest of my life!" she says.

"I'm sorry," I say again. "I feel better that I told you. I promised myself every day that I would tell you, but it seemed like my lie just got bigger, and I didn't know how to stop it. I should've just told you when it happened."

"You're better at lying than you said you were," she says, smiling.

"I know. I guess I am."

"I think I feel better that I don't have to pretend anymore," Darby says. "Do you?"

"Yeah," I say. "A lot better."

Then the bell rings, and suddenly Darby yells even louder than the bell, "I DREW THE PICTURE! I DREW THE PICTURE!"

Everyone who's running in from recess is stopping to look at us.

Darby looks at everyone staring at us and gets a big smile on her face.

"I . . . DREW . . . THE PICTURE OF . . . THE *DAVID* STATUE!" she tells them.

Her eyes are wide open.

Then I look at everyone, spread my arms wide, and yell, "I KILLED THE RAT!

Chapter 27
Jolly Good

I walk into class the next day like I have a dozen helium balloons tied to my back—I feel so light without my Big Bad Black Hole Lie.

I see Darby in the coatroom.

"I got my cast off!" she says, holding out her arm.

Her arm is all white with black hair on it.

"Eww," I say.

"It feels so light!" she says.

"Me, too!" I say.

We sit down for SHTV. The fifth-graders are holding up umbrellas.

"Today's weather is fifty degrees and . . . SUNNY!" says the girl.

They fold up the umbrellas and put on sunglasses.

"Gotcha!" they say, laughing.

They didn't really get us, since we can all see that it's sunny out, but it was funny anyway. Kind of. Maybe Darby and I will be funnier next year when we get to be on SHTV.

"Now," the co-anchor says, "Mr. Scott, our media teacher, will be telling us about an exciting opportunity."

Mr. Scott slides into the screen, also wearing sunglasses.

"Hi, kids!" he says. "I received an email from London, England, today that was forwarded to me by fourth-grade student Jill Johnson's dad."

I look at Darby. Oh, no. Is Jill coming back?

"It's a wonderful opportunity," he says. "There's an international contest to produce a short documentary video about the environment and the issues we face today. The winners of the contest will get to travel to London! If you're interested, please come visit me at lunch, and I'll tell you more about it!"

Everyone starts talking.

"If we win, we could go to London and see Jill!" Darby says to me and Iris.

"I'm not so sure about seeing Queen Jill," I say. "But going to London sounds like a good idea!"

"Jill's not our queen anymore, remember, Lily?" Darby says. "Besides, Iris would be with us, so she could remind us to think for ourselves. Right, Iris?"

Iris smiles.

"We could make it about pigs," I say. "Iris, you could help a lot, since you know about how eating pigs is bad for the environment."

And pigs are so CUTE!

"That would be fun!" says Iris.

"Let's do it, then!" says Darby. "We could tell the story about how we saved Bacon."

"Maybe we could even visit him at Hog Heaven," I say.

"Jolly good!" says Darby in a British accent.

"Lovely!" says Iris.

"My video will be the best," Deets says. "Besides, my dad has friends in Hollywood, so it'll probably even be made into a real movie."

We all roll our eyes. I think about how I felt walking around with a Big Bad Black Hole Lie on my back and how glad I am that I finally let it go. How does Deets just keep lying and lying? He must be walking around with lies clinging all over his body. It must make him super tired.

"You could help us with our video," says Iris.

"Really? ... I mean, maybe," he says.

"We need phones so we can shoot the video," I say. "Maybe I can finally convince Mom and Dad to get me a phone!"

"Good plan!" says Darby.

"I have the best phone!" says Deets.

"Really?" I say. "That'll be perfect."

Then Mrs. Larson gives us more exciting news.

"Class, I have something to share!"

"More rats?" asks Sonja.

"No, not more rats," says Mrs. Larson. "I think we're done with rats."

"What is it?" shouts José.

"A spelling bee!" says Mrs. Larson.

"Awwwwwww . . ." says everyone all at once.

"This is exciting!" Mrs. Larson tries to convince us. "I'll be passing out practice books for all of you. But not everyone has to participate. It's up to you."

I know I want to do it. I love watching the National Spelling Bee when it comes on TV.

"I was the best speller in my old school," says Deets.

Darby and I look at him. I think about what Dad said about how no one should be treated as badly by their dad as Deets is. I guess I'll just keep trying to be nice.

"We could study together," I say to him.

"I want to study with you, too!" says Iris.

"I guess me, too," says Darby. "I'm a good speller. R-I-Z-Z-L-E-R-U-N-K!"

"Can you use that in a sentence?" I ask her.

"RIZZLERUNKS RULE!" she says.

Then we all open up our math journals and start writing equations.